AMISH MYSTERY AT ROSE COTTAGE

ETTIE SMITH AMISH MYSTERIES BOOK 16

SAMANTHA PRICE

CHAPTER 1

NELL GRABER LOOKED out her second-floor bedroom window at her oldest son, John. He was walking beside the men carrying his father's coffin into the house. Soon the place would be full of people for the customary viewing.

The gentle rain falling drew Nell back to years gone by. The rain always reminded her of Jedidiah. How odd it would rain today of all days since they'd had none for weeks. It was as though the Lord had held back the rain and was sending her the message that

Jedidiah *was* safe. Was Jedidiah by His side, along with her beloved Abraham?

As any sensible and faithful woman would do, Nell pushed Jedidiah from her mind. Today was about Abraham, the man she'd spent over forty years with, and had five *kinner* with. It wasn't a day to ponder a lost love, but nearly anything could bring Jedidiah to mind. Today it was the rain, other times it was hearing a word he'd been fond of, or seeing a certain expression on someone's face. The lift of an eyebrow, or the just-so tilt of a head.

Gazing up at the gray clouds stretching across the early morning sky, Nell thanked God for nearly a lifetime with Abraham. It was a blessing *Gott* had snatched him away in his sleep, saving him from a slow and painful death. He had so many health issues that Nell had despaired when she'd thought about the future. In their early marriage Abraham had rarely been sick and he wasn't a person who did well in a sickbed. He was truly happy in the fields with the sun on his back and his hand to the plow, smelling the dirt and watching the crops grow. If he'd lived longer, his throat cancer along with his liver cancer would've had him confined to the house, or his bed. She shuddered at the thought. Even though she'd miss him, she was pleased he'd been spared the suffering of slowly fading away.

When she was twenty and first learned of Abraham's attraction to her she dismissed him, but only because he was many years her senior. Back then, a man of twenty-seven seemed so old. She covered her mouth with her fingertips and had a quiet giggle at being concerned about seven years. Seven years was nothing now. How silly she'd been back then to wait months before she accepted his offer of a buggy ride, but she hadn't been sure what had happened to Jedidiah. Abraham knew what was on her heart, and he was a patient man. They'd been seeing each other regularly for two months when he asked her to marry him.

She had agreed, and she had never regretted the decision.

Their five boys would be at their father's funeral even though only the older two had stayed on in the Amish community. It was Nell's hope the other three would all return one day and bring their families with them. Abraham had been her strength when their younger children had left the community. To her it was the worst thing that could happen, but Abraham reminded her everything was in *Gott's* hands.

Nell's sister, Jennifer, had made her a blue dress to wear today. It was a mid-blue tone, the same color as the dress she'd worn for her wedding. It was a kind gesture of her sister's. Nell pulled it from her wardrobe and slipped it off the wooden hanger. The original wedding dress had doubled as her

Sunday best and had worn out years ago. Had it lasted, it would've been way too small anyway. After so many years and five *kinner*, her size had increased. She wasn't the biggest woman in the community, but she sure liked her food and wasn't about to apologize for her appetite.

After she took off her cotton nightgown, she pulled on the specially made dress. The fabric was soft and didn't look as though it would wrinkle easily, which would be a timesaving blessing. After a quick look out the window, she noticed the hearse still there. John was most likely settling the bill.

Jennifer had made her a *kapp* and matching apron along with the dress, but Nell decided to wear Abraham's favorite *kapp* and apron—the set he'd complimented her on a few months back. They were relatively new and were also sewn by Jennifer, so her sister wouldn't mind that she chose to wear those instead.

After donning her apron, she walked across to her nightstand and took hold of her boar bristle brush and pulled it through her thigh-length hair. The brush was bought for her by Abraham on one of his rare trips to town. He never liked to go to the stores and only went there to purchase boots or tools. She remembered the way he'd presented her with that brush. He'd smiled as he told her it was made from boar bristles and would be good for her hair. It was their nightly routine before bed that Abraham would brush her hair in their bedroom. A special brush had been a delightful and thoughtful gift.

She placed the brush down on Abraham's side of the bed, and then divided her hair into two sections, tightly braiding each one before winding it and securing against her head. As she walked back to fetch her *kapp*, movement out the window distracted her. The funeral director and his helpers were walking out of the house, having done their job. Now, the community would take over and the coffin would be transported from her house to the gravesite in the bespoke horse-drawn funeral buggy.

There was a sudden knock on her bedroom door. *"Dat's* back, *Mamm."* It was John, her eldest.

"Denke. I'll be down in a minute." She sighed knowing she'd miss Abraham's smile, his warm embrace, and his constant support and encouragement. *"Gott,* please help me to get through this day." She left the window and was about to push open the door of her bedroom. Instead, she was pulled back to the window, back to the rain.

Even though she'd only been married once, she'd lost two loves in her lifetime. She lifted one hand to the window and placed her fingertips on the cold glass, causing a shiver to run through her body.

Since Abraham had left her, she'd had a constant pang in the pit of her stomach. She covered her tummy with her hand and knew it was the gnawing pain of being alone. Solitude—it was something she'd never liked.

Things would've been different if she'd had daughters, but she'd had all sons. Her granddaughter, Gloria, was now the closest person in her life, and she made up for having no daughters. But, nothing could replace the loss of a husband. Abraham had been there to cook for, and together they sat by the fire and read at night before going upstairs to their bedroom. They'd been so close, and now life would never be the same. It was hard to start anew and learn to live in solitude at this stage of her life. Starting over was for the young who were looking to bright futures, finding their way.

Looking up into the gray sky, she wiped a tear from her eye and then looked to the fields and trees on the misty horizon. There was a big undiscovered world out there. A world beyond the Amish community. If someone wanted to disappear they could do it so easily. That led Nell to think something she'd so often pondered; there were also innumerable places where one could hide a body. "Where are you, Jedidiah Shoneberger? Are you alive, or are you gone and your body's still out there somewhere?"

CHAPTER 2

THERE WAS something cozy about the rain and Ettie loved watching it fall and listening to the gentle pitter-patter on the roof. Afterward, the trees and the nearby pastures were always greener and fresher.

"Ettie, come away from the window. They'll see you for sure." Elsa-May continued her knitting as she spoke, sitting on her usual chair.

Ettie heard her sister babbling in the background. It was a constant noise, day in and day out. Elsa-May rarely had anything important to say and, when she ordered Ettie about in that older-sister way, it bothered her. Elsa-May should realize that once they'd reached adulthood, the older sister bossiness should've left. In Ettie's eyes, they were as good as equal now. After all, they were both in their eighties. Still, she wasn't brave enough to suggest that to Elsa-May, not yet.

"Did you hear me, Ettie?"

Ettie took a deep breath and had one last look at the house next door through the raindrops on the windowpane. "I heard you the first time. They won't see me."

"Come away." Her sister's voice was louder now.

"I need to see what they're doing." Ettie hoped if Elsa-May realized how fascinating their neighbors were to watch, she too would become interested. "He's moved the car to the bottom of the driveway, he's parked it, and now he's going back into the house. He isn't moving fast. It seems he doesn't care about getting wet. He doesn't even have on a coat, or a jacket. They're going somewhere. Where?"

"It's got nothing to do with us."

"I wouldn't be so sure. What if they're going somewhere to put in an official complaint about Snowy's imaginary barking? Or making a complaint about the fence?"

"Come, sit down and talk for a moment."

To the sound of the clickety-click of Elsa-May's knitting needles, Ettie watched their neighbors, Greville and Stacey Charmers, hurrying out of the house next door. "Wait, something's happening." Stacey was trying to put up an umbrella, and Greville was literally pulling her along. "What's the hurry, I wonder? Hmm, their last name's Charmers. There's nothing charming about them. Especially not him."

"What did you say?"

All Ettie wanted to do was watch them,

now that they were outside. And, why wasn't Greville waiting for Stacey to raise her umbrella? He was an intolerably rude man.

"Ettie. Are you listening to me?"

"I'm coming. Be patient."

"Sit down. We've got to talk about whether we're going to Abraham's funeral today. We don't have much time if we're going."

As Ettie moved to sit back down on the couch, her eyes traveled to the plain china clock on the mantle. It was a few minutes before nine. Elsa-May was right. If they were going to the funeral they had to get ready. "Hmm. I don't feel like going, not really. Not in this weather."

Elsa-May stared at Ettie while she continued her knitting and, as usual, never dropped a stitch. "There have been too many funerals lately. And I don't feel up to it."

"Are you ill?" Ettie half hoped she would

say, "Yes," so staying home with her older sister would be her excuse too.

"*Nee* I'm not, but I don't like going to funerals because I always wonder if the next one's going to be mine."

Ettie chuckled. Her sister had been saying that for years. "I think the real reason you aren't motivated is because Jeremiah's staying home to look after Ava with her morning sickness."

"She's past that stage. She's just feeling off. I remember the tiredness I felt when I was expecting. It's even harder when you have a few little ones to run after. Anyway, what you said makes no sense."

Finally, Ettie thought. "It does?"

"I said *no sense,* Ettie. Don't tell me your hearing's going."

"It does make sense, though. You like things the same all the time. You have your funny habits and you don't like change."

Elsa-May stopped knitting and her jaw dropped open. "I don't have habits."

Ettie chuckled. "You do. Ava and Jeremiah usually drive us to the funerals in their buggy, and now that they're not going to this one you feel uncomfortable."

"Don't be ridiculous. We always go everywhere by ourselves. Why would that bother me?" After she gave Ettie a disapproving scowl, she took up her knitting needles.

Ettie twisted the strands of hair at the nape of her neck and pushed them back into her prayer *kapp*. If they decided to go, she'd have to pin her hair a little better. "But we don't go to the funerals alone, just the two of us."

"I suppose not, but don't go making out I'm a nut case, or whatever you said about having habits. Everyone likes to have a certain routine with their life. It's not just me. You like to do the same things every day. You have the same breakfast, and ..."

Ettie shifted her position on the couch as she half-listened to Elsa-May drone on about what Ettie did on a daily basis. When she heard the next-door neighbors' car start up, she couldn't resist going over to the window and looking out. "They're only driving away now. That means they've been sitting in the car for minutes before they left. All that time we've been talking they were in the car not moving."

"Don't let them see you," Elsa-May hissed.

"I'm standing back away from the window." Ettie watched the back of the car as it traveled down their road. "He was dragging her to the car in the rain and not even giving her a chance to put up her umbrella. Come to think of it, he moved the car away from the house so she'd have further to walk in the rain."

"Hmm. Maybe they were having an argument about that once they got in the car."

"You might be right," Ettie said.

"There's something not right about them."

Ettie looked over at Elsa-May, who seldom agreed with anything she said. "Then you agree?"

"*Jah*, but it's not our business and it won't do any good you staring at them, especially if they see you. I don't want Greville coming over here complaining about you watching them. It's bad enough he's already complained about Snowy. I don't want him ever to have reason to come here again."

Ettie looked down at Snowy asleep in his dog bed in the corner of the room. He wasn't normally a barker and it was odd their grumpy neighbor complained that he barked while they were out. "I suppose you're right. I don't mind staying at home today." Ettie rubbed her chin. "I think I'll have a baking day today since we can't possibly leave the *haus*." Ettie knew if a member of their Amish community saw them, there'd be questions about why they hadn't been at Abraham's funeral.

"You should. You haven't baked for a while. Cookies?"

Cookies were fun to prepare and the house smelled wonderful once the cookies were baking in the oven. *"Jah,* good idea. I think I'll make a variety we haven't had in a while. I'll go through the old recipe cards and see what I can find."

"Want some help?"

Ettie was delighted her sister had offered to help in the kitchen. Normally, either one cooked or the other. "I'd like that."

Elsa-May put her knitting in the bag by her feet, and together they walked into the kitchen.

AFTER ETTIE and Elsa-May had confirmed

the decision not to go to Abraham's funeral, they retrieved the box of old recipe cards from the top shelf of the kitchen cupboard. With her large frame Elsa-May pushed Ettie out of the way, divided the pile of index cards into two, and then passed half to Ettie.

They both sat down at the table and began to leaf through the two stacks.

Pulling out a yellowed card, Elsa-May said, "Here's one for peanut butter cookies. Ah, I remember how *Mamm* got this recipe. *Dat* had them at someone's *haus* and asked *Mamm* to get the recipe."

"Was it for these cookies? *Dat* didn't like peanut butter," Ettie said.

"I'm certain it was these. *Jah,* I remember it as clearly as though it was yesterday."

Ettie didn't agree, but after years of living with her sister she knew it was best to keep quiet about the little things. She knew their father wouldn't have liked peanut butter cookies, and the knowing was all that mattered.

"Why is your face screwed up like that?" Elsa-May asked. "Don't you believe me?"

"Um, it sounds about right. Shall we make the peanut butter ones, then?"

"*Jah,* let's do it." With her glasses perched on the end of her nose, Elsa-May took another careful look at the recipe clutched in her hand. "We have all the ingredients."

"*Gut.* Let's get started."

Elsa-May passed the card to Ettie, who fetched all the needed items and placed them on the table while Elsa-May carefully folded her glasses and then looped them over the neckline of her dress.

Ettie sat down once everything was on the table. "You can measure the ingredients, Elsa-May."

Elsa-May stood and, as she dumped the measured items into the mixing bowl, she said, "Abraham was young."

The image of Abraham Graber popped into Ettie's mind. He had been tall, and his once jet-black hair had rapidly faded to white in the past few years, and that, along with his pale skin, had made him ill-looking.

Elsa-May added, "I hope Nell won't mind us not being there today."

"There'll be so many people there she likely won't even notice." Ettie handed Elsa-May a large jar of peanut butter, trying not to think about Abraham's funeral.

"I think she will, and you'll have to make up an excuse why we weren't there."

"I will make an excuse. I'll blame you. It was your fault. I was all set to go, but when you said you didn't want to, I decided neither did I."

"I mean, an excuse in case Nell inquires why we weren't there."

"Hmm. Maybe you could say you came down with a cold or something." Ettie chortled.

Elsa-May's mouth fell open. "I'll say no such thing and neither will you."

"Well, what will we say to her? We didn't feel like going because one day we'll be at our own funerals and we'll be dead and we prefer not to think about death until then?"

"Certainly not! I intend to go to others, I just wanted … I didn't want to go to one today. The truth is better than making up a lie. Once you start lying, it sets you on the path of a slippery slope. Then you have to keep making up other lies to cover up the first lie. Remember what *Dat* used to say?"

"Jah, 'if you're going to tell a lie, you have to have a good memory.' Or, something or other like that."

"That's right." Elsa-May shook her head vigorously, causing her prayer *kapp* to slip to one side. Ettie straightened it for her. Elsa-May gave a little smile. "It's a burden I'm not willing to carry."

"You're right."

"I usually am."

Ettie giggled, glad they were baking together and spending the rainy day indoors. Funerals in the rain were so depressing. Besides that, their boots would have gotten muddy, and then they'd have had to clean them when they got home. Out of all the routine chores, that was the one Ettie disliked the most. And Elsa-May didn't like it either, so Ettie couldn't even work out a swap.

CHAPTER 3

THE NEXT DAY, Ettie pulled a chair closer to the window. From there, she could better see what the Charmers were doing. Greville had left for work at his usual time of ten minutes past eight and Stacey had been out to water the flowers she'd planted three days before. It made no sense to water them now, since the soil would've received a thorough soaking from yesterday's rain. Ettie wondered if either of the two knew anything about gardening.

Even though Stacey had seemed okay

when they'd spoken with her, Ettie and Elsa-May kept away from her because Greville was so unpleasant.

As Ettie was trying to work out what kind of flowers Stacey had planted, out of the corner of her eye she noticed an unfamiliar buggy approaching. Her head swiveled as it turned into their driveway, and she looked to see who it was. It wasn't one of their frequent visitors or she'd recognize the buggy as well as the horse. "Elsa-May, someone's here."

"Who is it?"

"I can't tell yet." Ettie jumped when she saw who it was. Her stomach lurched and her heart pumped hard, and she felt almost as though she was going to become ill.

"Why do you look so bothered? Go to the door. You don't have to wait for them to knock if you've already seen them. And, they've probably seen you too, staring out the window like you have been doing." Elsa-May shook her head in disgust.

"It's Nell, Elsa-May."

Elsa-May's knitting fell to the floor as she jumped out of her seat with the gusto of a woman many years younger. "Nell?"

"Jah. What will we do?" Ettie hurried over to Elsa-May. "Should we hide and pretend we're not home?" Now Ettie wished they'd made the effort to go to Nell's husband's funeral. She could have convinced Elsa-May to go. Nell was no doubt there to express her disappointment, or to inquire if one of them was ill. So ill it prevented both of them from traveling the short distance to the funeral. Given the age difference of twenty years or so, they hadn't been close friends with Abraham and Nell, but they were close enough they really ought to have attended his funeral.

Snowy, disturbed by the panicked humans, got out of his bed, barked, and ran around in circles.

Elsa-May sighed. "We can't hide, Ettie, even if we wanted to."

"What will we say?" Ettie nibbled on the ends of her fingernails.

"I don't know. I feel dreadful. Now I know we should've— "

"It was your idea not to," Ettie said, even though she'd been first to say she just didn't feel like going out in the rain.

Elsa-May frowned, and opened her mouth to reply just as there was a loud knock on the door.

Ettie clutched at her throat. "Sounds like she's angry for sure."

Elsa-May took a deep breath and stepped toward the door. Ettie snatched Snowy just as he went to follow Elsa May, and put him out in the backyard. By the time she had closed the back door and clipped Snowy's dog door closed, Nell was already inside the house and Elsa-May was apologizing for not coming to the funeral.

Ettie stepped forward and looked into Nell's light blue eyes, made bluer by the same hues picked up in the dark dress she wore. Even though Nell was now in her early sixties, she still had the same dark hair she'd had in her youth, but now it was lightly salted with white strands. *"Jah,* we're sorry we didn't make it. We should've been there." Ettie hoped that was enough and no further explanation would be necessary.

"It went well. There were so many folks there. They came from all over the country. I came here today because I have a question to ask you both."

Ettie realized Nell wasn't going to ask them a question related to Abraham's funeral, and she could feel the tension in her body as it melted away. She must've let out a huge sigh because Elsa-May turned to her and pressed her lips tightly together. Ettie had to stifle a giggle at the *"Mamm* look" on her elder-sister's face.

Then Elsa-May's face switched to a pleasant expression as she turned back to Nell. "What is it you want to ask us?"

"Can we sit down?"

"Of course," Elsa-May said. "I forgot my manners for a moment."

"Come through to the kitchen and you can try our peanut butter cookies we made yesterday," Ettie said.

"That sounds nice. I am a bit peckish. I don't much like to eat alone, so I didn't have a real breakfast."

"And would you like a cup of hot tea?" Elsa-May asked Nell.

Nell nodded, and while Elsa-May and Nell were walking to the kitchen, Ettie couldn't resist another quick look out the window. When she had walked the few steps to the window, she was disappointed. There was nothing interesting to see. Stacey must've finished her watering and gone inside. Ettie quickly caught up with Nell and managed to sit down at the table at the same time. "What can we help you with, Nell?" Ettie asked.

"I was married for many wonderful years to Abraham."

"He was a good man," Elsa-May said while she noisily filled the teakettle with fresh water.

"Jah, he was. A very good man, but do you remember before I married Abraham I was set to marry Jedidiah Shoneberger?"

"Jah. That's right." Visions of the tall and handsome Jedidiah came to Ettie's mind. He'd been strong looking with broad shoulders.

"Did anyone ever find out what happened to him?" Elsa-May placed the teakettle on the stove and lit the burner beneath it, and then proceeded to place some cookies onto a plate. "Last thing I heard he was still missing." Elsa-May sat down with them and pushed the plate of cookies toward Nell.

"Denke," Nell said, as she took one.

Now it all came back to Ettie. No one had talked about it recently, but it had been the talk of the community for years. Jedidiah had disappeared without a trace right before he was due to marry Nell. "What happened to him?" Ettie asked while reaching for a cookie.

"That's just it. He was never heard from. At first, I thought he'd been killed, but his body never turned up anywhere. And who would have wanted to kill him?" She shrugged. "It didn't make sense. I knew in my heart he'd never willingly leave me. We were set to marry and he bought me Rose Cottage. He worked hard on it for weeks to make it a nice home." She sighed.

Elsa-May bit into a cookie and chomped loudly. "And you want Ettie to find out what happened to him?"

Ettie looked at Elsa-May, wide-eyed and totally surprised. How would she possibly find out what had happened to Jedidiah after all these years?

"That's exactly why I'm here." Nell grabbed Ettie's arm and Ettie jumped in fright at the suddenness of the movement. "Would you find out what happened to him for me, Ettie?"

"I'd love to help you, Nell, but I wouldn't know where to start. So many years have gone by."

"It won't be easy, of course, but Ettie will help you," Elsa-May said calmly. "Tell us everything you can remember. Think about what happened in the last days before he disappeared." Elsa-May raised her eyebrows and leaned forward to take another cookie while Ettie narrowed her eyes in frustration at Elsa-May for giving the poor woman false hope. And, for volunteering her help.

"I gave up on him coming back. Some old

ladies from the community suggested that *Gott* took him up to heaven without him dying, just as he did Enoch and Elijah in the bible." Nell sighed. "It would be nice if that were true. He was special to me, but he was just an ordinary man."

"*Jah*, that would be a good way for all of us to go," Elsa-May chuckled.

Nell didn't even smile at Elsa-May's comment. "After I married Abraham, I didn't want him to know I was still wondering what happened to Jedidiah, although, he'd have known how I felt about him. Everyone knew we were to be married. You can't just forget about someone you loved so much." She stared at Ettie, and Ettie nodded.

"It would've been so hard not knowing," Elsa-May said.

"It's always been at the back of my mind. It's been something that never left me. I thought I'd never know, but then yesterday it struck me. Who would I be hurting now if I resumed my search for Jedidiah? Do you understand what I mean?"

"Undoubtedly," Elsa-May said with cookie crumbs spilling out of her mouth.

Ettie grimaced and passed Elsa-May a napkin. *"Jah,* that would have put you in a difficult position, if you had looked for him while you were married. Where did you see Jedidiah last?"

"It was at Rose Cottage. It was the last place he was seen by anyone. He was working on it every day. He'd go to his regular job, then come home and do more work on the cottage, and then start again early the next morning. It was like he had two jobs."

Ettie cast her mind back to the old stone cottage. In her mind, she was sure Jedidiah bought the old place for them to live in after they married. Then Nell had ended up living in the place after he'd disappeared. "When did he buy Rose Cottage?"

"You're going to stay on there?" Elsa-May asked, talking over Ettie's question.

"*Jah*, they'll be carrying me out in a box." She smiled sweetly. "I'll never leave the place willingly."

Ettie and Elsa-May had been to the house many times.

"It's a lovely place and the rose garden is one of the best I've seen," Elsa-May said.

"It's not an easy climate to grow them in. I was fortunate that Abraham loved the roses too, and he loved the *haus*. Even in the last months when he was frail he'd never let anyone inside the rose garden, not even the *grosskinner*." Nell chuckled. "Especially not the *grosskinner* when they were younger. He insisted on doing all the work himself even when he became ill. To answer your question, Ettie," Nell continued, "Jedidiah bought the cottage a few months before our wedding date. I'd say it might have been ten or twelve weeks before."

"How did you come to own the place after he disappeared?"

"He bought it for me, and it was officially put in my name before he was gone. As I said, I was fortunate that Abraham loved the place as much as I did, and he never resented the fact that it had come from Jedidiah. Abraham moved in after we married and, as you know, we raised our family there. It's a special place to me."

Since her sister had volunteered their help, Ettie gathered some background information. Knowing he'd been last seen at Rose Cottage, that was where she began. "Why did he buy the place?"

"He knew I loved it."

Elsa-May said, "Forgive me for asking, but how did Jedidiah have so much money to buy Rose Cottage? I mean, he would've been so young, and you would've only been around eighteen I'm guessing?"

"Nineteen. He said he had all the money

and bought it outright, but my best guess is he borrowed money from an unscrupulous man. Because someone came looking for him twice when I was there watching the progress of the renovations. Jedidiah talked to him away from me, so I couldn't hear what was said, but the man had an angry face and was using threatening hand gestures."

Ettie and Elsa-May stared at each other. This might be the quickest mystery they'd ever had to solve.

"Jedidiah told me he had plenty of money, but looking back now I think he'd been trying to impress me. *Nee,* not impress, that's the wrong word."

"Make you feel secure?" Elsa-May asked.

"That's it." Nell's lips turned upward at the corners. The relevance of what Nell had just said about Jedidiah borrowing money apparently sailed right over her own head, and she continued, "*Jah,* he knew I loved the old place. Not long after he bought it he signed it over to me." Nell repeated, and then sighed. "He was fixing it up for us to live in, and one of the first things he did was to start replanting the old rose garden to make it look like it had when we were growing up." She drew a quick breath. "The *haus* was very old and needed a lot of work, though, so he left off the garden project and focused on just getting the *haus* ready to live in."

Ettie didn't think it would be likely that the man would run away after investing so much time and money into a house for them to live in after their nuptials. "Tell me this, Nell, who was the last person to see him?"

"The murderer, of course, Ettie!" Elsa-May said. The kettle whistled, and Elsa-May stood up to make the tea.

Ettie clapped her hands to the sides of her face in shock. "We don't know that he was murdered yet, Elsa-May. We have to deal in the facts, and all we know for certain is he disappeared." Ettie reached out and patted Nell's hand when she noticed she had been taken aback when Elsa-May mentioned murder.

Nell put her hand over her heart. "It's okay, Ettie. I feel, deep down, he was killed. It seems the only explanation, and that was the reason that I stopped looking for him. Otherwise I could never have married Abraham."

Elsa-May sat down. "His disappearance was talked about for many years. It's been the greatest mystery of our community."

"Even his family never had any word from him." Nell sighed. "Back then, I wrote to all his relatives. There was no one close, just second cousins and an aunt and an *onkel*. I've got a vague idea they weren't truly related, he just called them aunt and *onkel*. I wrote to them and everyone else I could think of. And every few weeks I put notices in the Amish newspapers."

Elsa-May leaned forward. "No one came

looking for him after he died? These unscrupulous men?"

"*Nee.* But there was only ever the one man. I never heard anything from him, and never saw him again."

"This man, how do you know he was unscrupulous?" Elsa-May asked.

"I've already told you."

Ettie asked, "You don't remember his name?"

"*Nee,* but over the years I've been trying to figure things out and this is my best guess. Jedidiah didn't know how fast he'd have to pay the money back that he'd borrowed to buy Rose Cottage. I know he didn't think much of banks because he'd made a few comments about them. I think he borrowed money from a private lender and thought we could pay the money back over twenty or thirty years." She shook her head. "I guess he wasn't good with that kind of thing. His parents, when they were alive, were very protective of him."

"I can understand why they were, under the circumstances," Ettie said, knowing about the miscarriages his mother had suffered. He was the only child who'd survived. "You need to tell us more, Nell. We need to know everything."

"I'm not holding back anything, Ettie. You ask anything you need to know."

"Do you have a loan on the cottage?"

"*Nee.* I own it free and clear."

That told Ettie the man wasn't there to have a loan paid off. Not a loan on the house at least. "What was happening around him the last day before he disappeared?" Ettie leaned forward to better hear Nell's answer.

Loud knocking on their door interrupted them. Elsa-May opened it to see Jennifer, Nell's older sister. "Jennifer, hello. Nell's here."

"I know. I figured she'd be here, by what

she said yesterday." Jennifer barged into the house, nearly stepping on Elsa-May's toes as she went right through to the kitchen. Elsa-May had managed to move out of the way just in time, and followed Jennifer into the kitchen. Looking over at Nell, Jennifer said, "So. There you are."

"*Jah,* I'm just talking to Ettie and Elsa-May—"

"About Jedidiah?"

"*Jah.*"

Elsa-May said, "Do sit down and join us, Jennifer."

Jennifer pressed her lips together, gave Elsa-May a nod and sat down next to her sister. "If you'd told me you were coming out here, Nell, I could've come with you."

"I didn't want to bother you."

"Anyway, continue what you were saying." She stared at Nell almost as though she were daring her to continue. Jennifer wasn't happy and everyone in the room knew it. Her presence had come with an atmosphere like a dark and threatening thundercloud.

"I was talking about Jedidiah, asking Ettie to help find him."

"You think he's alive, then?" Jennifer asked.

"I don't. I should have said, 'to find out what happened to him.'"

"Continue, Nell," Elsa-May said with a smile of encouragement.

"He was fixing up the place and our *bruder* was helping him." She shrugged.

"Which one?" Ettie asked.

"Our youngest *bruder,* Titus."

"We'll talk to him, if you don't mind," Elsa-May said.

"Of course, I don't mind. You can talk to him any time you want."

"And what else was Jedidiah doing?" Ettie asked.

"That was all. He worked on it all the

time. He was always there apart from when he was at his job installing drywall."

"And you can't think of anybody else who might have been angry with him? Was he having a feud with anyone?" Ettie asked.

"I had a feeling he couldn't be trusted," interrupted Jennifer. "Didn't I always say that to you, Nell?"

"Please, Jennifer, this isn't helping." Nell looked pleadingly at her sister.

Jennifer placed her hands in her lap and looked straight ahead.

Nell thought for a while and then shook her head. *"Nee.* I don't think so."

"Did you report him missing?" Ettie asked.

Her eyes grew wide. "Oh yes, everyone knew he was missing."

"I mean officially, to the police."

"Nee, I never went near them."

"Why not?" Elsa-May asked.

"I told her not to," Jennifer said.

Nell nodded. "We never had anything to do with the outside world. Things were different back then. Remember? We keep separate now, but I think things were much more that way back then."

Elsa-May said, "We'll have to get Kelly to look into things to see if there was —" Ettie grimaced and signaled to Elsa-May to be quiet.

Nell said, "That's okay, Ettie. You and Elsa-May don't have to be careful what you say in front of me. I've already come to terms with the fact he's dead. I feel he is dead, and you're right. I should've gone to the police to see if they had found an unidentified body. No police came around the community asking about a dead Amish man."

Jennifer shook her head. "I don't think he's dead. He's just gone away. He was a drifter. After his parents died there was nothing to keep him here. You've got to face it. If he cared for you he would've stayed."

Ettie noticed that Nell was hurt by her sister's unfeeling words.

Jennifer continued, "If he was dead someone would've found his body, and the police never came around asking questions."

"We'll see what we can find out for you, Nell," Ettie said.

"*Jah,* we will, and we're sorry again that we didn't go to Abraham's funeral yesterday," Elsa-May said.

Nell slowly nodded. "That's okay, don't feel badly. But I do hope I find out what happened to Jedidiah. I've prepared myself for the worst news. It's been awful never knowing. I thought about him every single day." She sipped her tea.

"I wouldn't go around saying that, Nell," Jennifer said. "You'll upset anyone who cared anything for Abraham, the *vadder* of your *kinner,* the man who stayed and faced his responsibilities."

Nell stood. "I should go. I've got visitors

this afternoon. People are stopping by before they go home."

Ettie stood up and walked Nell to the door. "Don't worry about a thing. We'll visit you in a few days' time after we've asked around."

"Or before, if we have questions," Elsa-May called out.

"Denke, for the tea and the cookies."

"You're most welcome," Ettie said.

Jennifer stood. "I haven't had any tea."

Ettie turned around to look at Jennifer. She had hoped she'd leave at the same time as Nell.

"Do stay for some, won't you?" Elsa-May asked sweetly.

"I'd love to." Jennifer sat back down while Ettie finished saying goodbye to Nell at the door.

Ettie noticed that Nell hadn't even said goodbye to her sister. Nell must've been dreadfully worked up by her sister's attitude, or upset with her for saying what she'd said about Jedidiah being unworthy of trust.

After Jennifer had a cup of tea in front of her and the attention of Ettie and Elsa-May, she said, "Tell me everything she said."

"She just asked us to find out what happened to Jedidiah, and you heard the rest."

"Cookie?" Elsa-May passed her the plate.

Jennifer looked down her nose. "What are they?"

"Peanut butter cookies."

"Nee." She took a sip of tea. "I'm sorry she came here to bother you. You must disregard anything she said. She'll bring shame on the whole family if she carries on with this nonsense."

"Aren't you curious about what happened to him? I mean, to Jedidiah?"

"Nee. It's none of my business except for him upsetting my *schweschder.* The reason I have never given two thoughts to his disappearance is because he simply ran away from

the responsibility of marriage. I don't know why other people don't see that."

"You never got along with him?"

"I did once, but that was back when we were young. The three of us used to play together, and then I was excluded."

"That must've been hard on you."

"*Nee,* it wasn't. I started to see his true colors." She took another swallow of tea and then stood. *"Denke.* I must go. Just don't waste your time on Jedidiah Shoneberger. He's not worth it."

ONCE JENNIFER WAS GONE, Ettie and Elsa-May cleared the cups, saucers, and leftover cookies, and then sat down again at their kitchen table. "Well, what do you think of that?" Ettie asked.

"What? The bossy older *schweschder* who was jealous of Jedidiah?"

"You think she liked Jedidiah too?"

Elsa-May shrugged her shoulders. "I'd say so. He was so handsome. Don't you remember?"

"I suppose he was, now you say so. And, as I remember, Jennifer married a little later than usual, when she was in her mid-twenties. She could've liked Jedidiah or could've been jealous of her sister's attention from him."

Elsa-May picked up a cookie she'd saved for herself. "She didn't even try a cookie. Did they taste all right to you?"

Ettie pulled a face. "Maybe the recipe's wrong."

Holding the cookie up higher, Elsa-May asked, "Do they look all right?"

"They do to me."

Elsa-May bit into another cookie, chewed, and then swallowed. "I can't taste much flavor."

"We should add more peanut butter next time. Maybe that explains why *Dat* liked them; they don't taste much like peanut butter."

After a huge sigh, Elsa-May said, "I always wondered what happened to Jedidiah."

"So did everyone."

"Where do we start?"

Ettie tapped her finger on her chin. "I think we should start by talking with Simon, Abraham's brother."

"Really? Why him? I thought you would've said Nell's *bruder,* Titus. He was working with him at the cottage."

"The reason is, I have vague memories of him liking Nell."

Elsa-May chortled. "I don't know how you could remember something like that from so long ago."

Ettie tapped her head. "I never forget a thing."

"What makes you think he'd know anything?" asked Elsa-May, totally ignoring her sister's comment.

"What if he wanted Jedidiah out of the way so he could marry Nell?" Ettie asked.

Elsa-May shook her head. "It was too bad for him, then, since she ended up marrying his *bruder,* Abraham."

"His plan didn't work."

"*Ach,* Ettie, you have a vivid imagination." Elsa-May chuckled.

"We have to start somewhere. Anyway, his place is on the way to the police station."

"Police?"

"Like you said, it won't hurt to have Kelly on our side with this. He can go back over the police records. Maybe there's an un-claimed body somewhere."

"That's true."

"So, I thought, on our way there we could talk to Simon."

"Ah, we're questioning people on a geo-graphical basis?"

"*Jah.*" Ettie scurried to the bureau in the living room, and pulled out paper and pen while Elsa-May let Snowy back in. "I'm writing down everything Nell said, so we can tell Kelly."

Looking at Snowy, Elsa-May sat down and grunted. "You'd better be a good boy and not bark. We won't be away for long. We don't want the neighbors complaining about you again."

"We sure don't." After writing for several minutes, Ettie folded the list and then poked it up inside her sleeve. "That's the last thing we need." Ettie walked to the front door, pulled on her coat, and took Elsa-May's off the hook by the door. "Ready?"

"*Jah.*"

"Take Snowy out the back now to do his business, so he'll last until we get home."

"He's just been out."

"Take him out again. Now we're getting our coats on he'll know we're going out. Just do it, Elsa-May, would you?"

Shaking her head, Elsa-May took Snowy out once more.

Ettie waited for Elsa-May and when she came back inside with the dog, Ettie passed Elsa-May her coat. They walked to the shanty to call for a taxi with Elsa-May complaining about taking Snowy out again, all the way there.

CHAPTER 4

THE TAXI PULLED up in front of Simon's house. They saw him sitting on the porch enjoying a midmorning mug of coffee. He stood up as they approached.

He gave a nod. *"Guder mariye."*

"Morning," Elsa-May said, as she strode in front of Ettie.

He fiddled with the neckline of his shirt. *"Wie gehts?"*

"We're fine, and you?" Ettie asked.

"Gut. Maizie's just gone out. You missed her by fifteen minutes."

"It's you we've come to see, Simon," Ettie said.

His face slowly contorted into a frown and with his thumb, he pushed his hat back on his head. "Me?"

In that moment, Ettie saw how much he looked like his late brother, Abraham. And that reminded Ettie he too had lost someone close to him, just as Nell had. It was a bad time to be asking him questions, but they were there now. *"Jah,* we want to ask you a few questions about Jedidiah."

"Jedidiah Shoneberger?"

"That's the one," Elsa-May said.

He tipped his head to one side, and looking from one lady to the other, asked, "Is he back?"

Elsa-May stepped onto the porch. *"Nee,* he's not. Mind if we sit?"

"Of course I don't mind. Sit down. I'll get another chair from inside." He turned to go in the *haus*. "Can I get you a cool drink, or anything?"

"*Nee,* we just had hot tea, *denke.*"

Elsa-May and Ettie sat on the porch chairs and then Simon sat down on the dining chair he'd fetched from the house. "Why are you asking about Jedidiah? I haven't even heard his name for years."

"We're trying to find out what happened to him. He was a good friend of yours, wasn't he?" Elsa-May asked.

"He was. Did Nell put you up to this?" His tone was sterner now.

"*Jah,* she wants to know once and for all what happened to him."

"She didn't wait long, did she?" He rubbed his beard, clearly bothered by his sister-in-law's timing.

"There's nothing wrong with that, is there?" Elsa-May asked. "He was her first love. That's not taking anything away from

Abraham. They had a *wunderbaar* life together."

"There's normally a certain adjustment process a person goes through after losing their spouse. That's all I'm saying."

"Oh, we're sorry. I think her grief over losing Abraham brought back the unresolved grief over Jedidiah. Is it too close to Abraham going home to *Gott* for you to talk about things like this?" Elsa-May asked.

He inhaled deeply. "*Nee,* it's okay."

"As I remember, you were keen on Nell, too, after Jedidiah disappeared, before Abraham made his intentions known." Ettie felt Elsa-May staring at her, obviously annoyed for bringing that to his attention.

"It's not a memory I'd like to go back to. I was interested in her, I won't lie. I was also interested in a few other women well before I met Maizie."

Ettie slowly nodded. "Do you know

where Jedidiah got the money from to buy Rose Cottage?"

"His parents."

Elsa-May and Ettie exchanged glances.

"Well, that's what I assumed. He had plenty of money."

"Is that right? Nell thinks maybe he borrowed money to buy Rose Cottage."

"*Nee,* he had money, and I'd say he'd inherited it. His grandparents on his *mudder's* side ran a dairy with hundreds of acres of land, and sold it for a huge sum of money. They also owned a lot of property around the place. He wasn't short of a dollar. He loaned people money, too. I'm surprised Nell doesn't know that."

Ettie's interest piqued when she heard he'd loaned money. It seemed Jedidiah kept that information from Nell. Perhaps he thought she wouldn't approve of him loaning people money. Had they gotten married, she would've known about his finances.

Although he might have chosen to discontinue making loans at that point.

"Do you have any idea what became of him?" Elsa-May asked.

He shook his head. *"Nee,* I don't."

"I know you write things for The Budget from time to time. Would you write something asking that if anyone has any information on Jedidiah Shoneberger, would they please write to me? Could you arrange that?"

"Jah. I'll get onto that immediately. I'll write the facts about how he disappeared and that people with any information can write to you."

Ettie gave him her address.

"I'll remember it."

"Denke." Ettie got to thinking. If Jedidiah had been killed, and he didn't like banks, where was all his money? Could that be a motive for murder? He had no family and he hadn't married Nell before he'd disappeared. No one seemed to think about his missing

money. And who had borrowed money from Jedidiah?

"Is there anything else you want to know?" Simon asked.

"Who borrowed money from him?" Elsa-May asked, taking the question that was on the tip of Ettie's tongue.

"And, was it a lot?" Ettie asked.

"That's something I'd rather not get into. It's between Jedidiah and the people who borrowed the money."

Elsa-May frowned. "It could be a clue to helping find him."

He shook his head. "It wouldn't help."

Ettie gave him a disapproving scowl, and when that didn't encourage him to give them the information, she asked, "Who else was he close with?"

"Titus and Moses. I know that both of them were helping him at Rose Cottage."

"And Abraham?"

"Abraham was a good friend, too, but he

couldn't help him work on the cottage because he was working long hours six days a week."

He was shying away from answering their questions directly. There was most likely no point trying to find out about something when so much time had passed. Ettie pushed herself to her feet. "We should keep moving. We've got to be in town for an appointment."

He stood also. "I've got business in town today. I can drive you."

"Are you sure?" Elsa-May asked.

"Jah. I was going in later, but it won't hurt if I go earlier. If you'll give me a moment, I'll just write a note to Maizie telling her where I'm going."

While he went inside, Ettie sat back down and whispered to Elsa-May, telling her the concerns she had. "He could've loaned money to someone who didn't want to repay. Knowing he had money, has given us a reason for his disappearance."

"You mean, his murder? Or, he could still be alive and he'd have taken his money with him?"

Ettie pouted. "I guess that's true. If he left, though, what caused him to go?"

"That's the mystery."

"If he was killed, where is his money? That's the other mystery. Like I said, maybe he loaned someone money and they didn't want to repay him? Didn't you hear me say that before?"

"*Jah*, but I didn't think it likely."

"Why not?" Ettie asked.

"It's our way that if we take a loan and if we don't repay, it's on our shoulders. If Jedidiah loaned money and it wasn't repaid, he would've forgotten about it. He wouldn't have asked for the money back."

Ettie nodded, knowing that there wouldn't

have been conflict over money between two people in the community. It was something that never happened. At least that door was closed. "Okay, you're right, so it's more likely that Jedidiah's money and the amount he had was not related to his disappearance or death?"

"That's what I think," Elsa-May said.

"Unless he loaned it to someone who wasn't in the community." Ettie sighed. "I'll feel better once we talk the whole thing over with Kelly. He might give us a prod in the right direction."

Simon stepped back onto the porch and placed his hat lightly on his head. "Are we ready?"

"*Jah,* we are." Elsa-May pushed herself to her feet and Ettie followed.

CHAPTER 5

ETTIE AND ELSA-MAY didn't want Simon to know they were going to speak with a detective, so they had him stop and let them out a few blocks from the police station.

"That was a bad idea," Elsa-May said when they had walked halfway to their destination. "It's so far."

"Think of it as your walk for the day since you didn't walk yesterday."

"I still have to take Snowy out when we get home."

"He won't mind going without for just one more day."

"I think he will, and if he goes without today, that'll make two days in a row. He likes his walks. You've seen how his little tail wags when he's prancing up the road."

Ettie and Elsa-May walked up the steps of the police station. Once they were just outside the door, Ettie said, "You do all the talking."

"Why me?"

"One of us has to."

"Okay. I'll do it. But if I forget something you jump right on in, okay?"

Ettie nodded and Elsa-May walked through the door first. Kelly was talking to one of the officers on duty at the front desk and he looked up, surprised to see them. "Mrs. Smith and Mrs. Lutz, what a nice surprise." His eyes crinkled at the corners indicating he was pleased to see them. And then his lips turned down slightly. "Is this a social visit?"

"We have something we'd like to discuss with you if we might," Elsa-May said.

"Certainly, come through to my office."

They followed Kelly down the long corridor that led to his office. He sat down behind his large desk, which was surprisingly free from the usual stacks of folders and paperwork. He clasped his hands on the desk, interlocking his fingers.

"Is it a slow time of year for you?" Ettie's eyebrows rose.

"It has been surprisingly quiet, and that's given us a chance to take another look at cold cases."

"That's fortunate because we've come here to talk to you about somebody who went missing around forty years ago."

His eyes opened wide. "Did you say forty?"

"Yes."

"Has he shown up?"

"No. He hasn't," Elsa-May chipped in, "That's the problem, you see."

"He's Amish?"

"Yes."

He opened his drawer and took out a yellow writing pad and clicked the end of the pen that he drew out of his pocket. "You better start at the beginning."

Elsa-May told him the whole story, and Kelly scribbled notes. "And that's everything we know."

Kelly looked at the two ladies and then read through the notes he'd penned. "He had no enemies that you know of?"

"Not as such, but there was that man who was harassing him, and Nell thought it was about the money he borrowed to buy Rose Cottage. Then we only just found out that he might have loaned people money, but we don't know who. You see, Nell's brother-in-law

Simon said Jedidiah was wealthy and hadn't needed to borrow. He had so much money he was able to loan money to other people."

Elsa-May said, "And we know it can't have been a private lender who came to harass him because he had a lot of money and didn't borrow on the property. Abraham's brother told us that."

"Let me see now. You said Simon is Nell's late husband's brother?"

"Jah. That's the one." Ettie was pleased he was taking them seriously.

"Hmmm, we could easily find out if a loan was ever registered against that property."

"You can do that?" Elsa-May asked.

"Yes. Now, scroll back a little. You said he loaned other people money?"

Ettie nodded and hoped he wouldn't ask more.

"To whom did he loan money and how

much was it?" He had his pen poised ready to take down the information."

Elsa-May said, "That's something we can't tell you."

"Only because we don't know," Ettie added.

"And why not?"

"Simon told us he loaned money to someone, or maybe more than one person, but he wouldn't tell us the details."

"Go back and try to find out." Kelly gave a quick nod. "And why didn't your friend report his disappearance?"

Ettie remembered that Nell's bossy older sister, Jennifer, wouldn't allow her to go to the police. It seemed she wasn't the only one who had a problem sister. "It was probably something she just didn't think about. We don't mix with outsiders, as you know, and even more so back then. We don't normally go to the police over things, we go to our bishop."

He clicked on the end of his pen a couple of times. "I'll do what I can, and I'll also check with the hospitals. I might need the name of your bishop from that time, too."

"Your help would be much appreciated," Elsa-May said. "We'll have to think back to who was bishop at that time."

They knew, but weren't sure why it was relevant.

He placed the pen on the table on top of the writing pad. "It won't be easy. It was a long time ago. All the hospital records are now computerized. They'll have to go back through their paper archives. He was in good health?"

"He certainly seemed so. He was working on the house, as we told you, with Nell's brother. He also had a regular job working for someone outside the community." Ettie pulled out the piece of paper from her sleeve and studied it making sure she'd told Kelly everything.

He leaned over. "What's that?"

"My list of facts. Yes, I think we've told you everything we know."

"See what else you can find out, and I'll see what I can find out from my end. You need to find out who would've benefited from him being out of the way. Either financially or socially, or any other way."

"There's no one that we can think of." Elsa May blinked rapidly. "He disappeared two weeks before his wedding."

"We're not sure if it was two weeks. It might've been one week," Ettie said.

"It was a matter of days," Elsa-May added.

Kelly waved a hand in the air. "My point is, did she ever marry after that?"

"Oh yes, she married Abraham Graber."

"He's only just died." Elsa-May added, "That prompted her to find out what happened to her first love."

He grimaced and looked down at his

notes. "Tell me more about this Abraham character."

Ettie looked at Elsa-May, but she just nodded, telling Ettie to tell the story. "He was a good man and a very quiet man. Abraham and Nell married several months after Jedidiah went missing."

"It was over two years, Ettie, before they married."

"Did he ever show Nell any interest before the man went missing?" the detective asked.

Elsa-May and Ettie looked at each other.

"I don't think so. Abraham and Jedidiah were good friends, weren't they, Ettie?"

"They were." Ettie kept quiet about Simon showing interest in Nell.

Kelly asked, "Abraham didn't wait too long before he jumped into his friend's place, did he?"

"I think two years is long enough, Detective. Nell tried hard to find Jedidiah. She must've written to every community in the country. No one had seen or heard anything from him."

"He disappeared off the face of the earth," Ettie added.

"There is always a trail," Kelly said. "I'll look him up on the computer now and see if I can find anything quickly. I'll run his name through the system."

"Thank you." At last, they might find out something. Ettie said a silent prayer, hoping something would jump out at Kelly.

They waited while Kelly tapped away at the computer's keys. "I can't find anything quickly. I'll get one of the officers to comb through."

"Thanks," Elsa-May said.

"What do you suggest we do now in our search for some answers?" Ettie asked.

"I'll start working on it from my end and you ladies find out what you can. Get back to me a couple of days." He stared at each of them until they nodded. "We'll go through the information and hopefully, we'll all have something to share." A slight smile turned the corners of Kelly's lips upward.

Ettie was taken aback. He rarely smiled unless he had food in front of him. Then she jumped a little when her sister dug her in her arm.

"Come on, Ettie." Her sister had just said goodbye to the detective and was standing up waiting for her to get up and join her.

Kelly stood. "Thank you, ladies, for coming in."

Ettie pushed herself to her feet. Kelly seemed pleased he had something to do.

As they walked out of the police station, Elsa-May said, "Did you see him smile?"

"*Jah*, I couldn't believe it. I kept staring at him."

Elsa-May carefully held onto the side railing as they walked down the front steps.

"It is intriguing; it's a big mystery, what happened to him."

"Oh, I do hope he's not dead."

"He's been missing for so long he almost has to be. Otherwise, Kelly was right about him leaving a trace, or leaving clues. All we have to do is find them."

"Is that all?" Ettie said with a trace of sarcasm as she shook her head. "It's going to be hard after forty years."

"Let's go to that coffee shop up the road and we can sit down and figure out who we're going to talk with next."

That pleased Ettie. She'd secretly hoped Elsa-May would suggest it. All the way there, Ettie's mouth watered thinking about the variety of cakes and pies on offer at the café. It had become one of her favorite places.

CHAPTER 6

ONCE THEY WERE at the café in front of the array of cakes, Ettie couldn't make up her mind. "So many choices."

"What do you feel like?"

"Something lemon and tangy. Do you think they'll have something like that today?" Ettie leaned down to look at the cakes toward the back. There were so many varieties it was hard to find the one she wanted.

Elsa-May shuddered. "That's the last thing I feel like. We'll have to have one each instead of sharing. Don't make me share today."

Ettie chuckled when she saw Elsa-May's look of desperation. "Okay, one each."

"You sit, and I'll find you a lemon cake or something tangy. It'll be my treat today."

"Really?" Normally Ettie paid, since she was the one with more money thanks to an inheritance from a friend. "Are you sure?"

"*Jah.*"

Ettie found a table near the back and sat down with her back to the wall. Normally, Elsa-May took that position, but today Ettie got to choose first.

While Elsa-May took her time in ordering, Ettie's mind wandered back to Jedidiah. Was he still alive, and had he gotten cold feet about marrying, like Nell's bossy-older sister, Jennifer, had said? Or, would his body turn up somewhere, someday?

Elsa-May pulled out the chair in front of

her, giving Ettie a smile. "I found you a lemon cake with thick frosting and lemon zest on top."

Ettie rubbed her hands together. "That's exactly what I feel like, *denke*."

Elsa-May put her change back into her small hand-sewn fabric bag.

"Did you order hot tea?"

"*Jah*, of course. Do you have pen and paper?"

Ettie pulled the paper out of her sleeve. "I have paper."

"No pen?"

Ettie shook her head. "No pocket for one."

"I'll see if we can borrow one." Elsa-May headed back to the counter, and came back a few seconds later with a pen. She passed it to Ettie.

"*Denke*." Ettie smoothed down the crinkled paper with the front of her arm.

"There's Titus, Nell's brother. Nell said he was helping Jedidiah with the house. They must've been spending a lot of time with one another."

Elsa-May shook her head.

"What's wrong?" Ettie guessed Elsa-May wanted to take charge, in her usual way.

"You're doing this all wrong. Let's start at the beginning. We already talked with Simon. Write him down and then cross him out."

That part didn't make sense to Ettie. Was Elsa-May trying to make the list look longer? They both knew they'd already talked with Simon. For the sake of peace and because she had decided not to fret over the small things, Ettie wrote down Simon's name and then crossed it out.

"Moses was a friend, wasn't he? A friend of Jedidiah?" Elsa-May asked.

"I can't remember who was friends with

him back then. I think everyone just mixed in together with one another."

"Write down Moses. We'll need to speak with him. I'm sure they were in the same circle of friends."

Ettie stared at the list. "Okay. And who else do we have?"

"We have Nell's younger brother, Titus, who was helping him at Rose cottage. Write that down."

"We wrote him first, before you made me write down Simon and cross him out."

The waitress arrived with a tray and unloaded their tea and cakes onto the table. Ettie's face lit up when she saw the small cake with the white frosting and the lemon zest sprinkled atop. It didn't matter that the piece was small, Ettie knew it would be full of flavor. Then her face fell when she saw Elsa-May's triple-layer chocolate cake with cream and ice cream on the side. "Elsa-May! Just look at that." She shook her head, worried about Elsa-May's health.

Elsa-May pushed out her lips. "You got what you wanted and I got what I wanted."

"That's why you offered to pay." Ettie refused to remind her for the fiftieth time she needed to cut back on rich food. At some point, her sister had to exert some self-control over her eating.

"Do you want some?" Elsa-May pushed the chocolate treat toward her.

"*Nee denke.* I'll stick with my lemon delight."

"Suit yourself."

Ettie inhaled deeply. "This is what we have so far. Abraham's brother, Simon. Then we have Titus, and Moses."

"That's a start."

"Not a very big one." Ettie placed the list down. "Nell said someone had come looking for him. I wonder who that was. It wasn't a man he'd borrowed money from like Nell thought."

"Not according to Simon, anyway. Perhaps Titus or Moses might know more?" Elsa-May broke off a portion of cake and popped it into her mouth. She closed her eyes as she savored it. "Oh, Ettie. Why is it that food that's bad for you always tastes so good?"

"You've got to train your brain to like different foods." Ettie put her cake fork through the frosting and collected some of the cake along with it. When she placed it into her mouth it was an explosion of tart lemon and sweetness—a delightful combination. "Oh, you've got to try this."

Elsa-May's lip curled. "I don't think it would go too well with the chocolate."

"Hmm, probably not." Ettie had a sip of hot tea. If there was a man angry with Jedidiah, he could've killed him and hidden the body. "Should we go to visit Titus after this?"

"I think we've had enough for one day, don't you?"

Ettie didn't want to put too much stress on her sister and they'd already been away from home for a good part of the day. "Okay, let's go home and we'll start again tomorrow. We'll need to stop by the markets and pick up something for dinner. We'll get some decent food after this indulgence."

"All right, we'll just pick up a few small things. Try not to buy things we already have."

Ettie frowned. "I only did that once."

Elsa-May stared at her and one eyebrow lifted just slightly.

"Okay, maybe I did it more than once."

Elsa-May's face finally broke into a smile. "We've both done it."

The chocolate cake had definitely changed her sister's mood for the better. Ettie took another bite of lemon cake and noticed Elsa-May was nearly finished already.

WHEN THEY GOT to the markets, they saw Ava getting out of her buggy.

"Ava," Elsa-May called out.

Ava looked over at them and waved.

They hurried over to her. "What are you doing shopping alone?"

"I always do. What are you two doing?"

"Shopping."

"Finding out about Jedidiah," Ettie said at the same time that Elsa-May had spoken.

"Jedidiah Shoneberger?"

"You know about him?" Ettie asked.

"I do. He went missing right before he was to be married to Nell Graber. Although, she wouldn't have been a Graber back then. I don't know what her last name was before."

"It was King," Elsa-May said. "Titus is her *bruder*, and he's Titus King."

"Ah that's right. I should have made that connection." As they continued into the markets, Ava asked, "What have you found out?

"Not much yet," Elsa-May said.

"Nell asked us to find out what happened to him."

"Did you end up going to Abraham's funeral?" Ava asked.

"Nee, we didn't."

"Nell came over to our *haus* the very next day and asked us to find out about Jedidiah."

Ettie added, "Just quietly, she didn't feel like she could investigate the matter while Abraham was still alive. Her sister came there too, after Nell had been there for a while, and she was quite annoyed that Nell had asked us. She thinks Jedidiah just ran away because he couldn't face marriage." Ettie touched Ava's arm. *"Ach,* you should've seen the look on Nell's face when her sister said that. She was devastated."

"Ettie! There's no need to tell people

something like that." Elsa-May shook her head and glared at Ettie.

Ettie gulped and was sad that her sister's chocolate-induced good mood hadn't lasted longer.

"I can't wait to tell Jeremiah you're trying to find out what happened to Jedidiah. I heard about him, but I haven't heard about him lately."

Elsa-May said, "I suppose you can tell Jeremiah we're looking into it. It's a big mystery and nobody seems to know anything."

"It's okay. I won't say anything to anyone but Jeremiah," Ava said.

They stopped by a vegetable stall and Elsa-May said, "We need potatoes, Ettie."

"I'll bag some."

Elsa-May turned to Ava. "As long as Jeremiah doesn't say anything, it'll be okay. I don't want it to be embarrassing for Nell and I don't want her to get in trouble from Jennifer."

"You don't need to say something like that to Ava because Ava won't say anything, and Jeremiah's against any talk or gossip of any kind." Ettie continued to fill the bag with medium sized potatoes.

Elsa-May nodded. "That's true. He takes after our *vadder.*"

Ava leaned against the stand. "Can I help with finding him?"

"There's not much to do so far, but we'll let you know," Ettie said.

"I'm just here to collect a few things; if you can wait I'll drive you home."

"Would you?" Elsa-May asked.

Before Ava could answer, Elsa-May turned to Ettie. "You get what we need and I'll stay with Ava."

"Okay." Ettie continued to look over the vegetables to see what else they needed while Elsa-May walked off with Ava. They had plenty of greens from their small but pro-ductive vegetable garden. All they really needed were carrots and potatoes, and a small amount of meat.

BY THE TIME Ettie paid for the vegetables and meat and got back to Ava's buggy, Elsa-May had arranged for Ava to drive them to speak with Titus the very next day.

CHAPTER 7

AVA STOPPED the buggy under a shade tree at Titus's house. It had been a long drive, as the Kings' farm was on the outskirts of the community. "You two go in and I'll stay here and rest."

"Are you sure?" Ettie asked.

"Mm-hmm. I don't mind sitting here. Take your time; don't rush on my account."

Ettie sat still and looked over at the well-cared-for house. "Titus and his wife mainly keep to themselves, don't they?"

"That's right, now that you mention it," Elsa-May said.

"Off you go," Ava said, shooing them away with hand gestures.

Elsa-May chuckled as she got down from the buggy. When they knocked on the door, Titus's wife, Sarah, opened it. She looked surprised to see them. They'd never visited her before, and it was too small a house to host Sunday meetings.

"Hello. Come in." She opened the door wider and smiled. Then she looked over at the buggy. "Is that Ava in the buggy?

"Jah. She's not feeling very energetic these days."

"She's around seven months along now, you know," Elsa-May added.

"Oh, could I take anything out to her?"

"She should be fine. We just came to see if we might have a quick word with Titus, if he's here."

"Of course. He was working around the

back. I'll see where he is now. Take a seat in here." She showed them to a small living room.

The curtains were drawn over the two small windows, leaving the room quite dim. Elsa-May sat and her eyes traveled to a framed cross-stitched sampler on the wall. She unhooked the glasses from her apron and popped them on the end of her nose. "Faith, Hope and Charity." The words were intertwined with vines. Ettie was looking closely at the sampler, wondering how long it had taken for someone to sew it, when Titus walked into the room.

"Hello, ladies. What can I do for you?"

Ettie pushed herself to her feet.

"Sit down, Ettie," Sarah said, as she came in right behind her husband. "I'll get us some hot tea."

"We don't need anything," Elsa-May said, "Unless you're getting something for yourselves."

"*Nee,* we're fine."

As Titus sat on the couch opposite to the ladies, Sarah said, "Do you want to talk to my husband about something personal, or of a private nature?"

"Not at all. You're certainly welcome to be here."

Sarah sat down, and Elsa-May continued, "We're here about Nell's ... well, we're here about Jedidiah Shoneberger."

"His disappearance," Ettie added.

Titus scratched the side of his cheek, and then squirmed in his seat. "What is it about his disappearance?"

Elsa-May looked directly at Titus. "We're wondering if you had any ideas where he might have gone."

"I was just as amazed by his disappearance as everybody else in the community. I have no idea what was going through his mind or why he left."

"According to Nell, you were one of the last people to see him."

"Was I?"

Elsa-May nodded. "That's right."

"I probably was. I was helping him at the cottage."

Ettie asked, "Doing what?"

"He wanted everything to be perfect before they got married. I think he had his head somewhere up in the clouds because there was too much to be done, far too much in the timeframe he had. The place was in a dreadful state. He wanted the *haus* and the garden both perfect. I told him it would have to be one or the other. I mean, a garden doesn't grow overnight. It made more sense to work on the *haus*."

"Quite right." Elsa-May nodded.

"Nell told me how she and Jedidiah used to walk past the place when they were younger and how much she admired the large pink and red roses. Then the place changed hands and was unlived in and unloved for years. I guess Jedidiah wanted Nell to have everything she'd ever wanted," Sarah said. "And have it all perfect." When Titus turned and frowned at her, she said, "Oh, well that's what it sounded like from what she told me. I never met him. I'm just going on what you told me, Titus, and what Nell told me."

Elsa-May asked, "Was he working in the garden or inside the cottage?"

"He took my advice and worked inside, mostly, after that."

"Was there anybody who was annoyed with him at the time?" Ettie asked.

He clicked his tongue. "I can't think of anybody who was ever annoyed with him. He got along with everyone."

"What about anybody who wished him harm?" Ettie frowned when she realized that was probably the same thing, but then she looked at Titus to see what he'd say.

He was silent for a moment, squirmed again a little as though his chair wasn't quite comfortable, and then he shook his head.

"Are you sure you wouldn't like a cup of tea or something? I do feel awful about Ava being out in the buggy by herself," Sarah said.

"It's our fault. She's driving us around today, but she's fine. It's too much effort to her to climb in and out, and we've just had a cup of tea before we left home," Elsa-May said.

Ettie nodded. "She's fine."

"What do you think happened to Jedidiah, Titus?" Elsa-May asked.

"I think he left of his own accord."

"Why would he do that?" Ettie asked. "If he was set to marry and had his whole life ahead of him?"

"I don't know. I think that's what he planned when he turned the house over to Nell. Why put it in her name if they were both to be married to one another?" Titus pressed his lips together. "He could've met someone else, or simply changed his mind about Nell. Otherwise, it makes no sense for a husband to put the house in the *fraa's* name."

Ettie noticed Sarah didn't look happy with his reasoning and that was confirmed when she scrunched her nose, and said, "I thought it was for the gesture. She loved the place, so he gifted it to her as an act of love."

Titus scratched his dark beard. "What is love? It's just a feeling. He might have gotten over the feeling when the reality of marriage set in. It was probably guilt over getting Nell's hopes up, and guilt over thinking about canceling the wedding that led him to give her Rose Cottage. It was better for Nell to have him disappear rather than for her to live with the shame of a canceled wedding. He was an honorable man."

"If that's what happened, it's the cruellest thing he could ever have done, to leave her wondering if he might be lying dead somewhere."

Titus turned to look at his wife. "Judge not lest ye be judged, Sarah."

Sarah let out a frustrated 'humph' sound. "Love isn't something you change your mind about."

"You don't know how the man felt, Sarah," Titus said. "No one does."

Sarah looked away from her husband. "You're right. I don't know Jedidiah, so I can't comment."

Embarrassed at the tension between husband and wife, Ettie cleared her throat. "We should go, Elsa-May."

"*Jah. Denke* for answering our questions."

As Ettie pushed herself to her feet, she said, "If you can think of anything that might help us in our search to solve the mystery, will you let us know?"

Titus bounded to his feet. "Of course, we will."

. . .

WHEN ETTIE and Elsa-May got back into the buggy, Ava asked, "What happened?"

"It was a little tense," Ettie said. "But, I did notice something odd. Sarah said, I don't know Jedidiah. She didn't talk about him in the past tense like everyone else does."

"It's just a word, Ettie. We didn't find out anything, Ava. Titus didn't know anything. He thought Jedidiah gave Nell Rose Cottage because he knew he was leaving."

"To appease his guilt over changing his mind about marrying her," Ettie added. "But, Nell never noticed anything amiss in their relationship."

"Well, it sounds like that was a waste of time. Where to now?" Ava asked.

"Back home, please," Elsa-May said. "By the time you take us home and then go home yourself, you'll be worn out. If you want, you can help us again tomorrow. If you feel up to it."

Ava nodded. "Okay."

As SOON AS Elsa-May walked in the door after their day with Titus, she looked around. "Where's Snowy?"

"He's probably outside," Ettie said as she glanced over and noticed the dog door hadn't been latched. Ettie and Elsa-May hurried to the back door and opened it, looking all around for Snowy. He normally greeted them when they came in the front door if he wasn't asleep in his dog bed.

Just as they stepped out into the backyard, a man's voice boomed from the front of the house. "You're finally home."

Ettie jumped with fright. "*Ach nee!* It's Greville." She went back inside to see that they'd left the front door wide open, and Greville was standing there holding out a grubby Snowy at arm's length. The normally fluffy white dog was all matted and covered in black dirt, and he was panting. He was almost unrecognizable except for his innocent dark eyes and slightly crooked bottom teeth.

"I've been waiting until you came home because this pesky dog ..." He thrust the dog at Ettie and she grabbed him. "This dog of yours pushed down the side fence, made his way into our place and left several messes over our newly laid lawn."

CHAPTER 8

ELSA-MAY WAS quick to take Snowy from Ettie and she held him close to herself in spite of the dirt because he was shaking in fear.

Then Ettie noticed that Greville was covered in dirt. "I'm so sorry he's gotten dirt all down the front of your lovely white shirt."

"It's not just dirt, lady, it's topsoil. It's expensive, and now I have to redo the whole thing. That'll take time I don't have, and money I don't have."

Ettie pulled her mouth to one side and

glanced at Snowy. "I'm terribly sorry, I don't understand how he could've done that."

Elsa-May asked, "How did he get into your place?"

"Take a look at your back fence. He's broken it down. You'd better get it fixed fast."

"Yes, we'll get it repaired immediately," Elsa-May said.

"See that you do. If your dog does anything like this again, I won't bring it back." He looked down at his shirt and dusted off dirt.

Elsa-May's eyes opened wide. "What do you mean?"

He pointed at Snowy. "If I see the dog on my property I'm going to take it to the pound."

"Why would you do that when you know he belongs to us?" Ettie asked.

"If you care about your dog, ladies, best you make sure he can't get out."

"We will," Ettie said quickly before Elsa-

May could open her mouth and say something that might further enrage him.

When Greville had stomped down the porch steps, Ettie closed the door. "He wins the prize for the most awful neighbor we've ever had."

"And then some," Elsa-May added, looking at Snowy. "What have you been up to?"

Snowy squirmed to get down.

"You can't let him down, he's covered in dirt. You need to give him a bath."

"I think the first thing we should do is take a look at that fence."

They closed Snowy in the bathroom, and walked out to look at the back fence. Two palings had been knocked over. Ettie was annoyed with herself. She knew the fence wasn't in the best repair and they should've strengthened it before something like this happened.

Elsa-May made tsk tsk sounds. "This is no good, no good at all."

"I think they'll be okay, they just need hammering back up. I can do that myself. You go inside and I'll get the hammer and the nails."

"Do you know what you're doing, Ettie?"

"Of course I do. You go and give Snowy a bath and I'll tend to the fence."

Elsa-May took a step back. "*Nee,* Ettie. It needs to be done properly."

Ettie pulled a face.

"I'll call Jeremiah to fix the fence as soon as I finish bathing Snowy."

"What makes you think I wouldn't do it properly?"

"I've seen how you drive nails in and you've never driven a nail straight in your life."

Ettie scratched her chin. "No matter. It'll still stick together even if the nail's a bit crooked, won't it?"

Elsa-May narrowed her eyes. "We need Jeremiah. If this happens again … you heard what Greville said he's going to do."

Ettie sighed. Her sister was right. She probably wouldn't do a good enough job of it. "Okay. I'll call Jeremiah while you look after Snowy."

"Good."

EVEN THOUGH IT wasn't cold enough to have a fire, Elsa-May didn't want Snowy to get cold. The evening air always had a slight chill to it. After she had scrubbed and rinsed him twice, and thoroughly dried him with one towel and then another, she lit the fire. Just then Ettie walked through the door. She'd been gone for some time. Ettie had only gone to call Jeremiah, remembered Elsa-May. She wondered what had taken her sister so long. "Did you get Jeremiah? Is he coming?"

"*Jah,* he and Ava are both coming over right now."

"What took you so long?" she peered at Ettie.

"I wasn't long at all."

Elsa-May could tell by the look on Ettie's face that she'd been up to something. "You were spying on them again, weren't you?" Elsa-May asked as she sat down.

Ettie's eyebrows rose so high that they nearly touched the edge of her prayer *kapp.* "Who?"

"Greville and Stacey."

"I don't spy."

"Whatever you choose to call it, you were watching them again." If Greville saw Ettie watching him, that would only enrage him further. Elsa-May wasn't used to angry people; they scared her. Especially Greville, who towered over both her and Ettie, to say nothing of his blazing, flashing eyes.

"I was simply talking to Stacey while she was in her garden. She apologized for her husband's behavior. I didn't know what to say. It would be wrong of me to agree with her that his behavior was dreadful, but it was. And she shouldn't be the one apologizing."

While Elsa-May listened, she got off the chair, and pulled Snowy and his dog bed closer to the fire. "You'd better make enough dinner for Ava and Jeremiah tonight."

"*Ach,* it's my turn again?"

"*Jah.*"

"I should've asked them if they could stay."

"They probably will." Elsa-May made herself comfortable knitting.

"Unless they have something else planned."

"We'll soon find out."

Several minutes later, they heard the sounds of buggy wheels turning on the gravel and the clippety-clop of hooves. Elsa-May opened the door in time to see Jeremiah helping Ava down from the buggy. Ettie rushed past her, almost sending her flying.

Ettie barely said hello to Jeremiah as she linked arms with Ava to help her into the house.

"I'm fine, Ettie," Ava said with a giggle.

"Are you sure?"

"Take a seat in front of the fire," Elsa-May said.

"I hope you didn't put that fire on for me, because I have a little furnace inside me keeping me warm all the time. I'm generally too hot."

Ettie said, "Snowy needed a bath after his adventure with the neighbor's topsoil."

"Oh no." Ava laughed.

When Jeremiah walked in the door, Ettie rushed over to him. "Come with me and I'll show you where the fence needs nailing back together."

"I'll go around the side so I don't get the house dirty from my work boots."

"Don't worry, it'll be fine. We've already got dirt on the floor from Snowy."

Jeremiah laughed as he walked through the front door and headed toward the back with Ettie.

"She wanted to fix the fence herself," Elsa-May explained with a chuckle.

Ava giggled. "Jeremiah's happy to do any work around the place."

"He's always been the one we can rely on," Ettie said.

"Me too," Ava said.

When Ettie and Jeremiah went outside, Elsa-May picked up the towel by Snowy's bed, kneeled down, and continued to dab at his damp fur. "I never like washing him late in the day because it takes too long for all his fur to dry."

"He'll dry by the fire. It looks like he's quite comfortable there."

"He's just happy to be out of the water. He doesn't like baths one little bit. Oh, I must show you what I've knitted for your *boppli*. I've also been knitting teddy bears for the children's hospital, so I've been busy."

Ettie walked back into the house. "Would you like to lie down, Ava?"

"I'm fine, Ettie. Sometimes I have a little sleep in the afternoon, but not every day."

"You can lie down in my room. Jeremiah might be a while fixing the fence."

"When I got home, I ate a lot and that gave me more energy. And I had a rest on the drive over. I can't wait to see what you've knitted, Elsa-May."

"Ah." Elsa-May got up, and headed over to the bureau. She leaned down and pulled out a fabric bag. It was the same bag where she kept all her special knitted pieces. Ava moved to sit closer when Elsa-May sat back down in her usual chair. One by one, she showed Ava the tiny clothes.

"Oh, Elsa-May these are lovely! They're so delicate. I don't know how you do this so well."

Elsa-May stretched her knobbly-knuckled hands out. "I might not be able to do it for much longer, so I'm making the most of it."

"I'll keep these forever and tell my children they came from their great *grossmammi,* and then they can be passed down through the generations."

ELSA-MAY SHOOK her head and made a funny sound, and Ettie knew she was pleased with what Ava had said.

"Have you made any progress with your thought processes regarding Jedidiah?" Ava asked.

To the sound of loud hammering outside, Elsa-May said, "We haven't had any time to think about things. When we got home, we were immediately faced with a broken-down fence, a cranky neighbor, and Snowy, who sorely needed a good scrubbing."

"Let me know if I can help you with anything besides driving you tomorrow."

"*Nee,* you've done quite enough for us," Elsa-May said.

"It would give me something to do. And I'd appreciate it. I haven't been doing much. Jeremiah won't let me do a thing."

Elsa-May chortled. "And neither should you do anything too ambitious, except rest and get ready for the birth."

"*Ach nee,* don't frighten me."

Elsa-May folded the baby clothes and placed them back in the bag. "There's nothing to worry about. Women have been giving birth for thousands of years."

"I know. That's something I keep telling

myself. Everyone else can do it, so I'll be able to."

"You'll be okay." Ettie said.

Ava gave a weak smile. "I'll feel much better when the time comes."

Ettie stared up at the ceiling. "I remember when I was waiting for my firstborn to come. I thought the day would never arrive."

"That's kind of how I'm feeling. It's taking so long." Ava's mouth turned down at the corners.

"I think you should rest and not go out tomorrow. You look tired and it's our fault."

"Nonsense. I didn't have to come back with Jeremiah just now. I feel fine."

"Ettie's right. You rest up tomorrow. We'll fill you in on what we find out. You must think of your *boppli.*"

Ava sighed. "Okay."

JEREMIAH OPENED THE BACK DOOR. "I've fixed

it as best I can. You shouldn't have any more problems."

"That's *wunderbaar. Denke,* Jeremiah," Ettie said.

"I hope that keeps your neighbor happy."

Ettie pulled her mouth to one side. "Well, that would be a hard thing to do."

"It's a wonder Greville hasn't come over here to complain about the hammering." Elsa-May chuckled. "He's caused us some problems since he moved in. But I'm sure he thinks we're his biggest problem."

"And our disagreeable yapping dog," Ettie added.

"That's true," Elsa-May said.

Jeremiah sat down with them. "Ava tells me you're trying to find out what happened to Jedidiah Shoneberger."

"Jah," Elsa-May nodded. "Do you know anything?"

"I don't. Ava and I were talking about it on

the way here. I don't think there's any use doing anything about it. If the man could've been found he would've been by now. Nell might find out something she doesn't want to know."

"Jeremiah and I don't agree on this," said Ava gently. "I said that Nell wants to find out, no matter what the truth is. I think that people can handle the truth, it's the 'not knowing' about a thing that's the hardest." Ava looked at Jeremiah. "If you'd gone missing two weeks before our wedding, I don't know what I'd have done. I don't know how Nell ever found it within herself to love again."

"She had to move on rather than live in the past, I'd say," Ettie said.

Elsa-May added, "She says she knew in her heart that he'd died. That helped her to move on. She wants us to find out why he vanished. There are so many unanswered questions, and she would like the truth."

Ettie nodded. "Who did he upset so much that they wanted to kill him?"

"Or did someone want to stop him from marrying Nell? Now, on a happy note, can you two stay for the evening meal?"

"I've got our meal prepared at home, but thanks anyway," Ava said.

"I don't know how you had time to prepare it," said Elsa-May.

"We have plenty," Ettie added. They would, once she cooked it.

Ava shook her head. "We're having a quiet dinner at home tonight. *Denke* for the offer."

CHAPTER 9

ONCE THEY STEPPED out of the taxi, Ettie had a look at Rose Cottage with fresh eyes. It was a little run-down looking, but that only added to the charm. Large roses, all shades of pinks and reds, still bloomed in the much-loved rose garden at the side of the house.

"Come along, Ettie. What are you staring at?"

"Just taking it in."

Elsa-May walked ahead and knocked on the door. Ettie caught up with her and waited by the scratched and faded turquoise-colored door. The narrow windows were framed in the same color. It was an odd color choice for doors and windows, especially for an Amish house, but somehow it suited the place. More subtle and neutral shades were preferred by the folks in their community. Nell wouldn't have thought twice about skirting the parameters of what was expected, but with Jennifer around it was surprising she hadn't 'suggested' her sister have all the doors and windows painted white, cream or beige.

Nell answered the door. "What have you found out?"

She looked at them so expectantly that Ettie felt awful to have to tell her they'd found out nothing.

"Nothing yet. We've come to ask you some more questions," Elsa-May said.

"Do come inside." She ushered them into her long narrow living room. On the end of the room there were two tall rectangular windows looking out onto the fields.

"You can see forever from here," Ettie said as she sat down.

"*Jah,* it's a lovely room. I like to sit here and knit."

Elsa-May's face lit up. "Ah, you like knitting?"

"I do."

"We're looking for more ladies to help us knit for the hospital."

"Someone else asked me to knit for something or other and I agreed, but I never heard anything else about it. I'd be very happy to help, Elsa-May."

Elsa-May's face beamed with delight and she asked Nell to make squares in a certain size. "I'll stop by soon and bring the yarn. I've had a lot donated by a store in town."

"Okay. It'll give me something to keep my mind occupied."

"Good. I told the lady in charge of the volunteers that I'd deliver a certain amount by the end of the month, and I'm way behind because I've been knitting for my newest addition to my family, Jeremiah and Ava's *boppli*."

"Ah that's right. She must be due soon?"

"Soon enough. Another couple of months."

"I'm so pleased to see the both of you because I'm having a big dinner on Friday night to show my appreciation to everyone. Everybody has been so good and kind to me after Abraham's death, and John has agreed to do some renovations on the house. I thought there's no better time to have a big get-together."

"Sounds great." Ettie knew that was a good opportunity to talk to people about Jedidiah, but only if she could slip it casually into the conversations.

"What are you having done to the place?" Elsa-May asked.

Nell placed both hands in her lap. "According to John, there's rising damp in the spare bedroom." John was her oldest son, in his early forties with a family of young adult children of his own. He was the only one of her five sons in this community. The second eldest had made his home in his wife's community, and the three youngest had all chosen to leave the Amish life.

"Is that on the eastern side of the house?" Ettie asked.

"That's right. The side near the rose garden. He will have to disturb the garden a little and Abraham would never have allowed it."

"That's good that John can do it for you. We have Jeremiah to do most things around our house. Everyone else seems too busy, but Jeremiah is always there on the very day that we ask him to do anything for us. He's a blessing of a grandson," Elsa-May said.

Nell sniffed. "I always feel a little guilty for getting the work done now."

"Why's that?" Ettie asked.

"Because Abraham would never do anything to the place. Nothing big. I saw the problems there myself years ago and he refused to fix anything."

Elsa-May looked around the room they were in. "The place looks freshly painted and in good repair."

Nell swiped a hand through the air. "He'd do things like that, but he didn't want anything else touched. And he insisted on doing everything himself. He wouldn't even let John help, even though he used to help out at John's *haus*."

"My husband was stubborn like that too," Elsa-May said.

Ettie's mind was on cooking. "Shall we bring anything to the dinner?"

"I'm having some of the ladies bring

desserts. Would you mind bringing an apple pie?"

Ettie asked. "What about something hot as well?"

"My *dochders*-in-law will be here all day helping me cook. Everything's under control."

"It sounds like you'll have a busy day and a busy night."

"And when is your son starting on the work?" Ettie asked.

"He's undecided whether he'll start on Saturday or Monday. If he starts on Saturday he'll have to stop for Sunday, but if he starts on Monday, he can work through the week."

ON THE WAY HOME, Ettie and Elsa-May stopped by Moses's house, but he still wasn't home.

Later that evening, as the sisters sat knitting in their living room, Ettie decided to talk about something that had been bothering her. "Elsa-May, I've got the weirdest feeling."

"Upset tummy?"

"*Nee.*"

"Your eyes probably need a rest."

"*Nee,* it's nothing like that. It's something Nell said."

Elsa-May lowered her knitting and looked over the top of her glasses at Ettie. "What's that?"

"What if Jedidiah was killed and buried at Rose Cottage?"

"Don't be silly."

"Well, I just got the weirdest feeling when she was talking about John doing renovations. And, remember how she keeps saying Abraham would never let anyone do anything?"

"*Jah.*"

"Well, don't you see?"

"You're just having flashbacks of what

happened at Agatha's house when her old beau was found under the floorboards."

"Do you think so?"

Elsa-May nodded. "There's no chance of anything like that happening again."

Ettie sighed. "You're probably right."

"There's no probability about my being right."

CHAPTER 10

THE FOOD WAS SERVED buffet style at Nell's special dinner for her friends. Ettie was pleased she could move around and now she'd have a chance to speak with Moses.

It was in the middle of the meal when she saw him across the other side of the room talking with a few people. She waited until the others moved on before she approached him. "Hello, Moses."

He nodded his head. "Ettie."

"How are you enjoying the food?"

"I've heard you been asking questions

about Jedidiah." He shook his head. "No good will come of you poking around in things like that. I know that's the only reason you've come to talk with me." Ettie opened her mouth to speak, but couldn't get a word in. "You need to leave things alone."

"And why do you think I would do that? Jedidiah has never been found and I was wondering if you know anything."

"Like what? You think I killed him? Is that it? And if I did, what reason would I have for that?"

"*Nee,* I don't think that at all, but —"

"Ettie, I don't want to be rude to a woman many years my senior, or any woman, so I'd be pleased if you never spoke to me about it or had anybody else speak to me about it ever again." He opened his eyes widely and all she could do was agree. He took his plate of food and strode away from her.

She'd never had an Amish person speak to her so abruptly or so dismissively. It made her feel terrible. She hurried over to tell Elsa-May.

"Ettie, what did you find out?"

When a friend came up to speak with them, Ettie whispered, "I'll tell you when we get home."

Elsa-May nodded, and Ettie was pleased that her sister didn't insist on knowing immediately.

After they had chatted with the friend, Elsa-May left to speak to someone else while Ettie sat down by herself on a chair at the side of the room. She had a good look around. Did one of these people know what happened to Jedidiah? Surely someone knew something, and if so, why were they keeping it a secret?

Was he killed for his money? Who were the people he'd loaned money to? Ettie still hadn't gotten to the bottom of that one. If he hadn't kept his money in a bank, where had he kept it? Was it still hidden in Rose Cottage somewhere? Had Abraham found it and that's why he didn't want anybody poking around his house? Perhaps it was hidden in a box underneath the rose garden.

John walked up to her and sat down. "How are you, Ettie?"

"I'm okay. I hear you're starting work on this place."

"Yeah. The state of it has been bothering me and my *bruder* for some time. *Dat* wouldn't allow us to do anything about it when he was alive. I think he was worried we might be neglecting our own homes by fixing his."

"Possibly. I could understand that. What are you going to do?"

"No drastic changes."

For the next ten minutes, Ettie tried to look interested while John told her what he was going to do to his mother's house. He hadn't even been born when Jedidiah disappeared, of course, and Ettie would much rather be speaking with someone who was old enough to remember those days. She'd asked the question, so she had to listen to the answer.

When he paused for a breath, Ettie made an excuse to leave and headed back to help with the desserts, which were now being placed on the table.

"There you are, Ettie." Elsa-May placed their pie and another pie on the table.

"Can I do anything?"

"It's all done." Elsa-May leaned in, and asked, "Did you find anything out from John?"

"Only what he's going to do on the *haus* here. He wouldn't know anything. I need to talk to older people. People who knew Jedidiah."

Elsa-May grabbed Ettie's arm and led her to a deserted corner of the room. "And what did Moses say? It didn't look like it went well."

"*Nee*. He was angry with us for trying to find out about things. He said we should leave things be."

"Hmm. We should take a closer look at him, then. He might know more than he's letting on."

"You might be right. No one else has been so upset with us for asking questions. A sign of a guilty conscience?"

"Maybe. I hope not, but, maybe."

IT WAS late Saturday afternoon when they heard someone pounding on the front door. "That's not Greville again, is it?" Ettie looked up from the square she was knitting.

They both looked at Snowy, fast asleep in his bed.

"He's been right there, asleep for hours. He hasn't done anything. Stay there, I'll see who it is." Ettie placed the knitting down even though she was in the middle of a row, and opened the door. She was quite surprised to see a worried-looking Ava.

"What is it?" Ettie's first thought was that it was something wrong with the baby. Elsa-May was by Ettie's side in an instant. "Is everything all right?" Elsa-May asked.

"We were at Nell's house just now and Jeremiah sent me to fetch you."

"What is it? Is it the *boppli*?" Elsa-May asked.

"*Nee.* They were digging by the house at Rose Cottage and uncovered a body."

Elsa-May let out a wail. "What?"

Ettie covered her mouth with her hand. It was just what she'd feared.

Elsa-May stared at Ettie. "It's just what you said."

Ettie nodded, speechless.

"Nell's asking for the both of you to come."

"How did you come to be there?" Elsa-May asked.

"We were there visiting her. We weren't at the funeral and we missed the dinner she had." Ava sighed.

Ettie rubbed her arm. "Are you all right, Ava?"

"*Jah*. I'm okay."

Ettie turned to her sister. "Come on. We'll have to lock Snowy inside."

"But what if he—"

"We can't worry about that now. We can clean it up later."

After they locked their dog in the house, the elderly sisters headed outside with Ava.

"I do wish Jeremiah hadn't sent you out like this by yourself." Elsa-May climbed into the buggy.

"I'm upset, naturally, but I'm perfectly fine. Jeremiah's helping John comfort Nell. She's near to hysteria, the poor woman."

"Oh dear. I suppose it was awful living

there the whole time thinking about where he was, and then to find out he was right there, near her the whole time."

"Where was he found exactly?" Ettie asked.

Ava took hold of the reins and clicked the horse forward. "I'm not sure. I just heard a man yell out. We were having a cup of tea with Nell, and Jeremiah ran out to see what the commotion was. He soon came back in with John. John told his mother what they found. Jeremiah sent me to get you, figuring he might be needed to help."

CHAPTER 11

WHEN THE THREE ladies arrived at the house, Elsa-May and Ettie stepped down from the buggy. They saw several men talking at one side of the house, and then they saw Jeremiah walking out of the house toward them.

"Have the police been called?" Elsa-May asked Jeremiah.

"*Jah,* they're on their way. Are you okay, Ava? Here, let me help you down."

She took his hand and stepped down from the buggy. "I'm fine."

Ettie looked down at the road. "They're

taking their time getting here if we arrived before them."

"John's only just called them now. I'll tend to the horse, and you go in and see Nell. She's not well."

"I'll stay outside," Ava said.

ETTIE AND ELSA-MAY made their way into Rose Cottage and found Nell sobbing into a tea towel at the kitchen table. John was beside her doing his best to comfort her. They both looked up at the sisters when they came into the room.

"I'll go outside and wait for the police, *Mamm.*"

"I'll be all right now. Don't go too far."

He gave his mother a little hug around the shoulders and then walked out of the room.

Ettie didn't know what to say. "Oh, Nell. You must've had an awful shock."

"It's dreadful. Absolutely awful."

"Tell us what happened."

She shook her head. "I knew it. I knew he was dead. Who could've killed him? I just don't know who could've done it."

"You didn't notice anything strange about the *haus,* or something different right after his disappearance?"

She was silent for a moment and closed her eyes. When she opened them she shook her head. "Not a thing. Everything was perfect, everything was in its proper place...well, apart from ..." she faded off.

"Apart from...?" Ettie leaned forward.

"It's just that I noticed a few tools were scattered here and there. Jedidiah was so adamant about always putting tools away in their proper place."

When Ettie heard a car, she stood up and moved to look out the window. It was the police. And behind the squad cars, Kelly was pulling up in his car. Ettie had to get to Detective Kelly and tell him that the body belonged to the man they'd been asking him about. That is, if he hadn't figured that out already.

Ettie turned to face Nell. "If you don't mind, I'll speak with the detective. He's the same one we've already spoken with about Jedidiah."

Nell nodded and Ettie went outside. She stayed back, not wanting to get in the way, but as soon as Kelly had taken a look at the scene she wanted to know what he thought. Besides that, she had no desire to see Jedidiah's remains.

When Kelly came finally came around to the front of the house he saw Ettie. "Don't tell me this is your man who went missing?"

"It is."

Kelly pulled a face. "We still have to go through the necessary steps to officially identify him. Where can I get hold of his relatives for DNA samples?"

"He doesn't have any close relatives, and not many distant ones."

"That's no good. We'll have to go down the road of dental records."

Ettie hoped Jedidiah had been to a dentist, otherwise it could be difficult to identify him. She kept quiet about that, not wanting to upset Detective Kelly. Not when he was being nice for a change. "His clothes?"

"Covered in dirt. It appears to be work pants and a plain shirt. No ID."

"Nell's in the house. Mrs. Graber, I should say, if you want to speak to her. She's very distressed. Do you have to speak to her right now?"

"I'll just ask a couple of questions, if she's not too distressed."

"We'll find out. Follow me." Ettie walked to the front door. As soon as they were at the door, she turned to the detective. "Do you remember the whole story?"

"I do."

"Well?" Ettie stared at him, prompting him to repeat it.

His lips pressed together showing his disapproval. "She was never married to Jedidiah Shoneberger but he bought this place, put it into her name, then disappeared. Never to be seen or heard from again. She lived here and then married Abraham Graber."

"That's right." He had been listening. Ettie showed him inside. "Nell, would you be able to answer some questions? This is Detective Kelly."

"Oh, Ettie said you've been helping her. Thank you."

"Mind if I sit down?" Kelly had his hand on the back of a chair.

"Please do."

"We'll leave you to it," Elsa-May said.

Nell grabbed her hand. "No, please stay with me."

"Is that all right?" Ettie asked.

"Sure," Kelly said as he sat down. He went

over the facts with Nell and she told him everything she'd already told Elsa-May and Ettie. "That should do it for today, but I'll need to ask you more questions later."

"Okay." She nodded.

"Do you have people who can stay with you?" Kelly asked.

"Yes, I'll have one of my granddaughters stay with me for a few days. They do a good job of looking after me."

The detective nodded. "That's good. The technicians will be working here for a few more hours. I don't want anyone crossing the police tape, even after they've finished." He turned shot Ettie a look.

"I don't want to go anywhere near it." Tears welled once more in Nell's eyes.

When Detective Kelly was finished, Ettie walked him out of the house. "What do you think?" Ettie asked him quietly.

He scratched behind his ear. "We need to find out who his enemies were."

"Does that mean you want our help?"

"'Help' is a strong word, but I would like you to keep asking questions. You've got a much better reach into your Amish community than I could ever have."

"You didn't find a gun or anything like that?"

He shook his head. "We weren't that lucky." When another car pulled up, he looked over. "Ah, that's the medical examiner now. I'll need to speak with him."

Ettie followed the detective. "Now we've got some direction. Now we know he was killed for certain. We just have to find out who did it and why."

Over his shoulder, he said, "I'll talk to you soon, Mrs. Smith." Kelly picked up his pace, so Ettie headed back to Nell.

Ettie and Elsa-May stayed with Nell for the next few hours until Gloria, Nell's oldest granddaughter, arrived.

CHAPTER 12

ETTIE AND ELSA-MAY had gone to the Sunday meeting the next morning to find that Nell wasn't there, and John and his family weren't there.

As the sisters walked back into their house after being brought back by Jeremiah and Ava, Elsa-May said, "Nell's taking this really hard. If only we could make her feel better in some way. She's obviously still very upset about the whole thing."

"And who wouldn't be? I can't think of

much else that could happen that would be worse than a thing like this."

"Me either."

A short time later, Ettie was sitting down and resting from their big day at the meeting when she saw Maizie pull up in a buggy. "We've got a visitor, Elsa-May." She opened the door and waited for her. "Maizie, this is a surprise. Come inside."

"I'm troubled about something, Ettie. I didn't want to mention it to you at the meeting."

"Who is it?" Elsa-May called out from the kitchen.

"It's Maizie," Ettie yelled back.

Elsa-May came out of the kitchen drying her hands on a cloth. "Maizie, what's the matter? You look dreadful."

"I feel dreadful."

"What's wrong?"

"I hate to say what I'm thinking out aloud. But, since you've been asking about

Jedidiah and I know you're trying to put the pieces together, I thought I should tell you what I think about how he died."

"Wait until I make the tea, then," Elsa-May said. "You will stay for some, won't you?"

"I will. I don't even want to speak the words I've come to say."

"Practice saying it in your head before you say it out loud," Elsa-May said. "I've got a pot of hot tea almost ready. Ettie and I were just about to have some."

They followed Elsa-May into the kitchen and then the three of them sat around the small circular table. Ettie leaned over and poured the tea for the three of them.

"Sugar or milk?"

"Just a little milk," Maizie said, and Ettie pushed the milk jug toward her. She poured a little into her cup and stirred it. "There. That's fine."

Maizie slowly took a sip of tea and then

carefully replaced the cup onto the saucer. "Lovely, *denke.*"

"Now, what's this dreadful thing you have to tell us?" Elsa-May asked.

Maizie swallowed hard. "I figured out what happened."

"What happened to Jedidiah?"

"*Jah.* I know who might have killed him and I hope I'm wrong."

"Who did it?" Ettie asked.

"I hate to say it, but I think it might've been Abraham. I couldn't tell my husband something like that about his *bruder,* and I couldn't tell Nell, but it makes sense."

Elsa-May drew back quickly. "Abraham?"

Maizie nodded. "It makes sense," she repeated. "He never allowed anybody to do any digging around the house or the rose garden. Nell told me that herself. You see, if anyone had been helping Abraham repair the place, they would've stepped on the body in the rose garden because I heard that Jedidiah wasn't buried that far down. Do you see what I mean?"

"Maybe Abraham just liked his roses," Ettie said, hoping that was the reason.

"You didn't see what he was like when anyone went near that garden. I don't like to think of it, but it might be true."

"Why would Abraham kill Jedidiah?" Ettie asked.

Elsa-May shook her head. "I can't imagine him killing anyone."

"Abraham liked Nell too. The two men liked Nell and she chose Jedidiah. When Jedidiah disappeared, Abraham was there to comfort her. Do you see where I'm headed with this?"

"Do you really think that Abraham would be capable of doing it? Killing is against the ten commandments. Thou shalt not kill," Elsa-May said. "I just can't see it."

"*Nee*, I don't think he'd do it. Not in my head." She tapped her knuckle on the side of her head. "Not the Abraham I knew, but what if he had an evil, dark side no one ever knew about?"

"Nell knew him better than anybody and she doesn't think this, does she?" Ettie asked.

"She's said nothing. I couldn't bear it if I found out that he'd done this dreadful thing, so I can imagine how she'd feel if it were true. It would've been better if Nell had never asked John to start on those repairs. They should've kept well away from the rose garden."

Ettie didn't know what to say. She was certain Abraham wouldn't have done something so dreadful. "Weren't Abraham and Jedidiah friends, along with Moses? I'm certain I remember them being friends."

Maizie nodded. "They were. Anyway, I just thought I should tell you. Then I can feel better."

"*Denke.* I'm glad you told us."

Ettie and Elsa-May both walked her to

the door. Then they waited until she drove her buggy away before they looked at each other.

Elsa-May sighed a long sigh. "Well, what do you think?"

"It's too horrible, but I must admit it crossed my mind," Ettie said.

"Me too."

"I suppose we can't rule it out." Ettie stood and watched Maizie's buggy getting smaller.

CHAPTER 13

ETTIE HAD TAKEN up her knitting again after the visit from Maizie. She was sitting in the seat by the window to keep an eye on what was happening in the street. Then a familiar white car came into view. "Elsa-May, it's Detective Kelly."

"What do you think he's found out?"

"You think he's found out something?"

"I do."

Ettie put her knitting down. "At this rate, we'll never get the knitting finished and ready for the hospital."

"It'll be late. Perhaps we could start with a few less than I told them, and make it up later."

As soon as Ettie opened the door, Kelly said, "I've got news."

"Ah, I was right," Elsa-May called out.

"You better come in and tell us," Ettie ushered him into the house before the neighbors could see him there again. She didn't want them to wonder why a detective was at their house so often. "Elsa-May just made a lovely cinnamon cake. And by just, I mean last night, so it's fresh. Would you like some?"

He rubbed his nose. "I don't mind if I do. No one can match your cakes or your sister's either."

Ettie gave a little giggle, but she knew they weren't the best bakers in the community.

When Kelly was seated in their living room with a plate of cake and a cup of tea, he began, "Yesterday, I did some digging."

"What did you uncover?" Elsa-May asked.

"Digging at Rose Cottage?" Ettie asked, imagining him with shovel in hand behind the police tape in the rose garden.

Kelly laughed. "I mean, I looked into some things a little deeper."

"Ettie knows that. She's not that daft."

Ettie kept silent. She'd keep to herself what she'd thought.

He raised his eyebrows and glanced at Ettie. "Good to know. I tracked down Jedidiah's old boss, Edgar Upton. Jedidiah worked for him on a pretty consistent basis. Jedidiah also worked with others, but Edgar was his main employer. I uncovered something that I believe to be significant."

"What's that?" Ettie asked.

"Edgar had a moderately successful drywall business and in his spare time he was involved in crime. He'd been in and out of prison for years. Two months here, six months there—"

"What kind of crimes?" Elsa-May interrupted him.

"Robberies, break and enters, that kind of thing. He was also a police informant for your old friend, Detective Crowley. Turns out this man, Mr. Upton, was the cause of five men in a bank robbery syndicate being arrested and doing time. With Edgar's information, these men were caught red-handed."

Ettie tried to connect the dots. "What does that have to do with Jedidiah?"

"Ah, well, I'm getting to that. It's a long shot, but where there's a disappearance there's often a link to criminals. I'm thinking there might have been a case of mistaken identity. I'm only about to tell you this because all of the people concerned are dead except for Edgar."

"Do go on." Elsa-May sat on the edge of her chair.

"Edgar gave up the information I just mentioned, he begged the authorities to put him into witness protection, but the powers that be didn't think it was warranted. After all, these men were bank robbers and they had no history of violence. What if one of these men put out a hit on Edgar, and Jedidiah got in the way somehow? It could've been a case of mistaken identity."

"I see," Ettie said, running the scenario through in her mind.

"And have you spoken with this Edgar man?" Elsa-May asked.

"I have questioned Edgar Upton. He lives in a retirement home. He's elderly but he does have all his faculties. However, Edgar Upton is keeping quiet on the whole thing. My gut tells me he knows more than he's letting on."

"Could we talk with him?" Elsa-May asked.

"I'm just putting the idea forward as a

possible scenario of what could've happened to your friend, Jedidiah. Can I ask if you've come up with any possibilities of your own?"

Ettie shook her head. Things were going slow. They didn't have any possible suspects yet.

"More tea?" Elsa-May said leaning forward and picking up the teapot.

"No, thank you. I've had quite enough tea today." He took another bite of cake.

Ettie knew not to ask him which nursing home Upton lived in because he'd ignored Elsa-May's question. Kelly wouldn't have told her anyway, and she knew Elsa-May was thinking the exact same thing. "Is that all you found out? Did you find any unidentified bodies, or bodies that were unclaimed back then?"

"None matching your fellow's description, or the timeframe. Are you sure you haven't found out anything you're keeping from me?" He narrowed his eyes at the two of them.

Ettie shrugged her shoulders. "We've come up with nothing."

"Drawn a blank," Elsa-May added.

"That is disappointing. I'm still following a few leads, so let's keep in contact, shall we?"

"We will," Ettie said.

"Thanks for the tea and the cake," Kelly said as he rose to his feet. "It wasn't too sweet and it was moist. Not sure it was one of my favorites, though."

"Oh, we'll keep that in mind," Ettie said. "We'll fix you something else next time."

The sisters showed Kelly out and when he had driven away, Ettie closed the door and turned around to face Elsa-May. "Notice how he kept saying the man's full name?"

"Edgar Upton. *Jah,* I did. Almost as though he wanted us to track the man down.

He even told us he was in one of those live-in retirement homes."

"We just need to call some local retirement homes. He didn't mention traveling a long distance."

"Let's look in the phone book, and then we'll walk Snowy down to the phone box and start calling."

THE THIRD PLACE they called confirmed they had a resident by the name of Edgar Upton. Ettie inquired about the possibility of visiting him. When she was done, Ettie replaced the phone's receiver and turned around to look for her older sister, who was walking Snowy up and down the road.

"Elsa-May," Ettie called as she waved her over.

"Did you find him?"

"I did. He's at Dreamy Meadows."

"With a name like that it sounds like— "

"I'm sure it's a lovely place and we'll find out soon enough because we're going there right now."

"We are?"

Ettie nodded. "You take Snowy home and I'll call a taxi."

CHAPTER 14

ETTIE AND ELSA-MAY walked up the ramp at the entrance of Dreamy Meadows.

"This is convenient, Ettie, no stairs. The name reminds me of a place for retired horses, though."

Ettie giggled. "The ramps are because they have old folks here and they might be in wheelchairs or walking with walkers."

When glass sliding doors opened as they approached, Ettie said, "We could do with a door that opens like this. It would be convenient."

Ettie walked up to the lady behind the reception desk and Elsa-May stayed back a distance. The place looked a little bleak, with mustard-colored carpet, white framed generic landscape pictures on the walls and a blue geometric-patterned wallpaper. It looked like nothing had been changed in fifty years, although it did look clean.

The receptionist stood up, glanced over at Elsa-May and smiled at Ettie. "Are you looking for a placing for your mother?"

Ettie opened her mouth in shock, realizing the lady thought Elsa-May was her mother. Then she could barely keep the smile from her face.

"We're not that old yet," Elsa-May said, not fully hearing the question.

Ettie leaned closer to the woman. "Actually, I think we are old enough to be in one of these places, but my sister and I are not here for that. We called earlier and asked about visiting Edgar Upton."

Elsa-May pushed Ettie out of the way. "Edgar Upton. Where will we find him?"

The receptionist glanced at the clock on the far wall. "It's eleven o'clock and that means he'll be in the games room. I'll take you there if you like; it's not too far."

"Yes please," Ettie said.

"I'm glad it's not too far because I'm so old," Elsa-May muttered loud enough for Ettie to hear.

Ettie frowned at her sister. She must've pieced together what the receptionist had said.

They were led down a wide corridor, and the second door on the left opened up into a large open space continuing onto an outdoor patio. "This is our games room. Most of our residents gather here before and after lunch."

"Which one is Edgar?" Ettie asked, looking around the sea of faces.

"He's right over there, the fellow in the green checked shirt."

"Thank you," Elsa-May said.

They walked over to the man she'd indicated. He was playing a game of chess with another man of a similar age. Edgar was a small wizened man who looked a little mischievous.

"Excuse me. Are you Edgar?" Elsa-May asked as she leaned toward him.

His face beamed. "I am, but you don't have to yell. I'm not deaf." He looked at Ettie and then Elsa-May.

"Oh, I didn't know I was."

"It's just her normal voice. I'm Ettie Smith and this is my sister, Elsa-May Lutz. We've come to ask you about a man you once knew."

"Jedidiah Shoneberger," Elsa-May added before Ettie had a chance.

"We're after a little information about him," Ettie explained.

Edgar looked away from them and his

gaze fixed on the man opposite. "Can we continue this later, Doug?"

"Humph. I was losing anyway. Maybe I should thank you two." The man gave the ladies a smile and moved his wheelchair away.

There was a nearby chair that Elsa-May pulled to the spot Doug had vacated, and Ettie sat on the one next to Edgar.

Ettie said, "We're both friends of Jedidiah and the woman he was set to marry. We're trying to find out what happened to him."

"Why have you come to me? Do you think I killed him?" He laughed nervously and covered his mouth with his hand.

Ettie didn't know if he knew that Jedidiah had been found buried at Rose Cottage. Jedidiah's name hadn't been officially released. They stuck to the story that he'd disappeared. "We don't think that, but there's a theory going around that some bank robbers might have killed him thinking he was you."

"Bank robbers?" Edgar threw his head back and laughed and then started coughing. After a guttural throat clearing, he said, "No. Jedidiah was most likely killed by the man he bought his house from. Either that or he ran from him in fear of his life. That man wasn't going to give up until that place was his again."

"The house? Do you mean Rose Cottage?"

"Yes, that was the name of it. Jedidiah wouldn't stop talking about it and the plans he had for it. It was the strangest thing, no sooner had he bought it than the previous owner wanted it back. He even ended up offering double the price, but Jedidiah still wouldn't sell. At that point, the guy got really mad. I told Jedidiah he should sell it back and buy something bigger and better, but he reckoned his girlfriend had her heart set on that place."

"Why did the man want to buy it back from him?"

"That's what Jedidiah asked me. He wanted me to see if I could find out for him. I found out, but then he never came back to work. When I went to Rose Cottage to tell him what I'd learned, no one was there. It happened right at the time of my jail incident."

"You were in jail?"

"No, not me, not then. Other people were in jail."

"Oh." Ettie wondered if the man was in his right mind because he wasn't making much sense.

"Well, what was the reason the man wanted to buy it back? Was gold or oil discovered on the land or something?"

"As good as gold, but not for Jedidiah. The only person the land Rose Cottage sat on was valuable to was the man who sold it. You see, the land was almost like a right-of-way to the corporation that wanted to buy the rest of the man's land. He didn't know it at the time, obviously, when he sold it. But when the corporation came knocking on his door he soon found out he needed the land back. The corporation didn't want it without that parcel of land that led to the road."

Elsa-May and Ettie exchanged glances. What the man said had started making more sense. "Surely the land must've had other roads that accessed it?"

"Do you remember what the man's name was?" asked Elsa-May, right overtop of Ettie's question.

"I'm sorry that's something I don't remember." He tapped his finger on his head. "I've usually got a pretty keen memory."

"You knew, then, that Jedidiah had disappeared?"

"I did. I found the woman he was marrying at the cottage about a week later and she told me he'd gone missing. I called back a few months later to see if he was coming back to work, but she said he'd never returned. Then she told me about a man who had visited him a couple of times. I knew that the man she'd described was the man trying to buy the land back. I didn't tell her that. Jedidiah hadn't told her, by the way she was talking. He probably didn't want her to worry."

"He's been missing all this time and that's been a lifetime of worry for her." Ettie nibbled on a fingernail.

"And he worked for you, is that right?" Elsa-May asked.

"How do you know that? Who have you been talking with?"

"You just said that," Ettie told him.

"We've been asking around because we've been trying to find out what happened to Jedidiah."

The man nodded. "If you want to know what happened to him, I just told you. He was either killed by that man who was trying to get his house back, or he ran in fear for his life."

"But he wasn't the true owner of the house," Elsa-May said.

"Who wasn't?" he asked.

"Jedidiah only owned it for a short amount of time before he signed it over and put it in the name of the woman he was to marry."

"Yes, I told him to do that."

"Why's that?"

"So he wouldn't be in danger of being killed," Edgar said.

"Wouldn't that put Nell in danger, then?"

"Who's Nell? The woman he was supposed to marry?"

"That's right," Ettie said.

He shook his head. "I can't remember. That's all I can remember."

"You've done very well," Ettie said, pleased they'd gotten that much out of him.

All they had to do now was find the man Jedidiah purchased the property from.

"I think it was something to do with him not having anyone to leave it to, and I said he should do a will before he married. He said he'd give it to her. Would either of you ladies care for a game of chess?"

Ettie shook her head. "No thank you. We don't play."

"We should go. Thank you for speaking with us," Elsa-May said as she stood up.

"You weren't here long. It's not even lunchtime yet. Will you come back and visit me again?"

"We might," Elsa-May said with a smile.

"If you come again, can you bring me some licorice?"

Elsa-May chuckled. "Yes, we will."

On the way out of the building, Ettie asked, "Why did you agree to bring him licorice? That means we'll have to come again."

"That won't hurt, will it?"

"I suppose not, but I just didn't think you'd want to with all the knitting we have on our plate."

"It wouldn't hurt. He might have no one else to bring him some, for all we know."

"Okay, we'll buy some next time we're at the markets. You can learn how to play chess in the meantime, and we'll come back to see him."

Elsa-May pulled a face. "I don't want to learn it. It's a game based on strategic warfare, if you didn't know."

"Well, you said we'd come again."

"I was just trying to be nice. It wouldn't hurt to visit again and bring him licorice."

Ettie sighed. "It's out of our way. Anyway, forget all that. Wouldn't Edgar have told Kelly what we just found out?"

"Possibly. Kelly doesn't tell us everything, you know."

"*Jah,* I do know that."

. . .

ELSA-MAY AND ETTIE had the taxi let them out at the bottom of their street. They wanted to call Kelly from the telephone before they walked to their *haus*.

"Hello, Detective Kelly, it's Ettie."

"Is everything okay?"

"Yes. We visited Edgar Upton." Ettie paused waiting for Kelly to tell her it wasn't a good idea to stick her nose into things. When he said nothing, she said, "Aren't you going to say anything?"

"What did he say?"

"You're not mad that we visited him?"

"Mrs. Smith, I can't stop a private citizen from talking to another citizen."

That was news to Ettie and a welcome relief. "He said that someone was angry with Jedidiah because he wouldn't sell them Rose Cottage."

"Who was it?" Now, he sounded interested.

"The same man who sold it to him."

"He wanted it back?"

"That's right." Ettie went on to explain what Edgar had told them. By what Kelly said, Ettie knew Mr. Upton hadn't told him any of that. "You can find out who owned it before Jedidiah can't you?"

"Yes. I'll be looking into it. Thank you, Mrs. Smith."

"I do wish you'd call me Ettie. Don't you think we know each other well enough by now?"

There was silence at the other end of the phone. "Mrs. Smith suits me fine."

"No one calls me Mrs. Smith. No adult does, anyway." In the background, Ettie heard someone calling the detective.

"I've got to go. I'll be in touch, and thanks again."

A loud click sounded in Ettie's ear.

"What did he say, Ettie?"

Ettie replaced the receiver and put the coins in the honesty box. "Not much really.

He thanked me a couple of times and I don't think Edgar told him any of what he told us."

"He can find out who sold Jedidiah the cottage?"

"Yes." Ettie sighed as she started walking home.

"What's wrong?"

"I can't help feeling like we're missing something."

"We're missing a whole lot of somethings. We might never find out who killed Jedidiah. All we can do is try, for Nell's sake. Let's just put the whole thing out of our minds and have a night where we don't talk about Nell, or Jedidiah, or what the Charmers are doing."

Ettie looked up at the Charmers house. There was no sign of them, and the car that usually sat in the driveway wasn't there.

"I can hear your brain ticking over, Ettie. Can we just have one evening of peace?"

Ettie nodded. "Okay. I'll put all my attention into knitting some more teddies."

"That's what I like to hear. The sooner we get the first lot off to the hospital, the better I'll feel."

CHAPTER 15

AFTER A QUIET AND peaceful evening followed by a good night's sleep, Ettie and Elsa-May woke early. When breakfast was over, Elsa-May took Snowy for his usual walk and, while her sister was gone, Ettie sat at the window where she could view the Charmers' house. They hadn't even said a polite thank you for fixing the fence that was shared between the two properties.

Ettie rubbed her chin and considered pointing out to them that the fence was co-owned. Maybe things were different where they came from. Although, Ettie couldn't imagine that they would be. The more Ettie thought about it the more she thought it was the right thing to do to inform her neighbors that the fence was owned between them both. Snowy got through the fence because it was so old and, unless they put a new fence up, it might happen again. Perhaps a stronger, better quality fence would be best —a higher one.

As Ettie was pondering what kind of fence she'd like, Greville's car pulled into the driveway. Then both Greville and Stacey got out of the car. While Greville went inside, Stacey got bags out of the trunk. *They've been away.* If Ettie hurried, she'd be able to talk to Stacey before she got inside, and avoid Greville altogether. Ettie was already dressed for the day except for her shoes, which she grabbed from by the door. She slipped her feet in and quickly did up the laces. Then she opened the door, walked out, and ran right into Detective Kelly.

"Oh, I'm so sorry," Ettie said.

"Where were you off to in such a hurry?"

"Nowhere." She looked past him to Elsa-May who was nearly back from her walk with Snowy.

He followed her gaze over his shoulder to Elsa-May, and then he turned back to Ettie. "I'll wait for your sister to get here. I have something to tell you both."

"Come in and have a seat." She stepped outside, so he could walk in and then she motioned for Elsa-May to hurry. "Quick, he's got something to tell us."

"I'm hurrying." Elsa-May walked briskly up the few steps of the porch, then walked Snowy through the house, saying a quick hello to Kelly. Once she had closed Snowy in the backyard, she sat down with Ettie and the detective.

. . .

"Is it bad news?" Elsa-May asked when she saw Detective Kelly's face.

"It's not bad news, it's surprising news. It was a shock for everyone. I've just come from Nell Graber's house and now I'm here to tell the both of you."

Both ladies sat still while Kelly inhaled deeply. "It's not Jedidiah. The body we found at Rose Cottage is not the body of Jedidiah Shoneberger."

Elsa-May gasped loudly, and Ettie couldn't believe what she was hearing. "Who is it then?" Ettie asked.

"We had dental records of a man who went missing around the same time as Jedidiah. His name is Arnold Salisbury."

"Who is he?" Elsa-May asked.

"Now this part gets interesting. He's the same fellow who sold Rose Cottage to Jedidiah. I had two reports handed to me at the same time. One was the identity of the previous owner of Rose Cottage, and the next one was the identity of the body found at Rose Cottage. They were one and the same, Arnold Salisbury."

Ettie leaned back. "The man who wanted to buy it back, and there are witnesses that he was harassing Jedidiah. That means that Jedidiah could still be out there somewhere —alive."

"He wouldn't have stayed away this long, Ettie." Elsa-May shook her head.

"There is that possibility, Mrs. Lutz. Perhaps he killed this man, buried him and fled."

"Jedidiah would never do anything like that. No one in our community would."

"There is a very real possibility that it happened just like that. You need to prepare yourselves for whatever will unfold."

"That explains why the man didn't harass Nell when she took ownership of the property. He was dead."

"How did Nell take the news?" Elsa-May asked.

"She was shocked like both of you, but she was a little sad that her question still remains unanswered—what happened to Jedidiah Shoneberger? Now, I'm more interested than ever to find him." Kelly clenched his jaw.

Ettie didn't like the sound of that, nor did she like the predatory gleam in Kelly's eyes.

"Keep in touch and tell me if you find out anything, okay?"

A few seconds after they agreed, Kelly was gone.

"Ettie, we must visit Nell."

"We should go there now."

"I'll just bring Snowy back into the house and get him a drink of water. That walk made me thirsty, so he must be thirsty." They kept Snowy's water in the house, just inside the back door.

CHAPTER 16

W HEN THEY GOT out of the taxi at Rose Cottage, Ettie saw the yellow police tape was still up. It was an awful sight, and it must have made Nell feel even more upset.

Nell met them at the front door with Gloria alongside her. "You heard?"

"Jah, Detective Kelly just came by and told us."

"I don't know if it's a good thing or a bad thing. I was so sure it was Jedidiah."

"We all were," Elsa-May said.

"The man was killed. Who killed him?"

Nell clutched at her throat and her grand-daughter put her head on Nell's shoulder and wrapped her arm around her grandmother's waist to comfort her.

"The detective will find that out. Don't worry," Ettie said.

They stayed at Nell's house for a couple of hours, making sure she was okay.

WHEN THEY GOT HOME, Stacey was waving at them as they were walking up their front steps. She was waving a piece of paper. When she got closer, Ettie saw it wasn't just a piece of paper, it was a letter.

"I've got this for you. I saw it hanging out of your mailbox, and I thought it might blow away. I thought it best I keep it safe until you came home."

The envelope had been opened and there was no sender's name and it just had the word 'Ettie' on the front. Ettie pulled the letter out and read, "Jedidiah is alive."

"That's nice to know. I couldn't help reading it too. Who's Jedidiah?" Stacey asked.

Elsa-May said, "A friend of ours who went missing many years ago."

"I hope you find him."

"Thank you." Elsa-May was doing all the talking because Ettie was in shock at Stacey opening her mail. "What did this woman look like?"

"She was small and she looked ... I'd say, middle-aged. She left her carriage down the road and came the rest of the way on foot."

"It's a buggy," Elsa-May corrected. "Did you notice if she had light hair or dark hair?"

"I couldn't tell. I'm sorry. She was too far away, and she was wearing a bonnet like yours. I was gardening and I didn't want to look as though I was staring at her. I don't think she even knew I was there. She popped the thing in your mailbox, looked up at your house and then hurried back to her buggy."

"What color was the horse?" Elsa-May didn't even start to explain about prayer *kapps*.

She shrugged. "Brown? I think. I'm not really sure. It just looked like any other buggy horse. I'm sorry. If I'd known it was so important I would've taken more notice."

"Thank you. We appreciate all you've told us," Ettie said, finally finding her voice.

"I better get back to cooking Greville's dinner. He demands it to be on time, or there's no telling what he'll do." She shook her head and then turned from them.

Elsa-May stood watching Stacey head back to her house and then, once she was halfway home, Elsa-May caught up to Ettie. "What do you think, Ettie?"

Ettie pushed the front door open. "I think we need to find the person who wrote this note. They'd know a lot more than this. I mean, how did they find this out?" Ettie looked the note over carefully turning it this way and that. "It's just a plain piece of paper written on with ordinary black ink."

After she sat down on her usual chair, Elsa-May pulled out the white baby shawl she was halfway through knitting. "It was a woman. All we need to do is—"

They were interrupted by a knock on the door. Ettie opened it to see Stacey standing there with another note. "I'm sorry, I forgot to give you all of it. That part fell out on my floor."

Ettie took it from her and saw the words. "Meet me in the park behind the library at two in the afternoon on Friday." She looked up at Stacey. "Thank you. This is very important."

"I'm glad I rescued it for you because it could've blown away. I hope it all works out for you and your friend."

"Thank you, so do I." When Ettie closed

the door, she looked over at Elsa-May, who was still knitting while looking at her over the top of her knitting glasses. That always amazed Ettie, as she couldn't knit well enough to lift her eyes from her needles.

"What is it, Ettie?"

"It's the rest of my mail. It says to meet her at the park behind the library at two on Friday."

"Him or her?"

"A woman delivered it. It'll be a woman we're meeting. You say the strangest things sometimes. Why would you think we'd be meeting a man? Stacey saw a woman."

"There's no name, that's all I was thinking."

"I'm not happy with Stacey thinking she can open our mail. I hope she doesn't make a habit of it. I just didn't know what to say to her."

"I don't think it's something that will happen all the time. As she said, she just happened to look up and see her putting something in our mailbox and it was sticking out far enough it might fall to the ground." Elsa-May came to the end of the row, turned the knitting around and started a new row.

"Any good neighbor would have popped it back in the letter box properly. Not done what she did. She took it back to her place and read it. What if she hadn't brought it back to us? Maybe we should get a lock on our mailbox."

"I don't think that's something that will ever happen again."

"I hope not. I thought Greville was the one to watch, but maybe she is."

Elsa-May gave a laugh. "We can't be suspicious of everybody. He's just got a bad temper and she's nosey, but so are you."

Ettie's mouth turned down at the corners. "I'm not being suspicious. Look what she did. It's something that people just don't do. You don't take something out of someone's mailbox and read it and then take it home with you."

"I agree it's a little odd. The main thing is, we might be getting closer to finding out where Jedidiah is, and hopefully he's still alive."

Elsa-May's brow wrinkled. "Who wrote the note?"

"We can guess all we'd like, but we'll find out tomorrow." Ettie placed the notes down on the side table and headed to the kitchen to prepare the evening meal. She secretly hoped the person wasn't going to tell them that Abraham did it, but what could he have had against Salisbury? Unless Salisbury came back looking for Jedidiah.

CHAPTER 17

THE NEXT DAY Elsa-May and Ettie were in the back of a taxi heading to the park. Elsa-May put a hand over her chest. "My heart's beating so fast."

"Mine too. I just hope this isn't a waste of time, or a prank."

"I don't think it would be."

"What if no one shows?"

"Of course they will. She took the trouble to write the note, and she hand-delivered it, so of course she'll be here."

The taxi pulled up at the entrance of the

park and they paid and got out. Then the two ladies wandered down the tree-lined path and sat on a bench in front of a small fountain. "She should see us here."

"It's not a large park."

They knew they had arrived ten minutes before two o'clock because that's what the taxi driver told them. They waited and then waited some more.

"It must be half past by now," Elsa-May grumbled some time later.

"Be patient. She might've been caught in traffic."

"Perhaps it was a prank. People like to play pranks. It was in the paper and someone probably saw it." Elsa-May rose to her feet. "Well I don't find it funny and if I find the person who wrote that note to you, I'll be giving them a piece of my mind." When Elsa-May turned away from Ettie, Ettie noticed an Amish woman entering the park from the other side.

"There's someone now, Elsa-May."

Elsa-May swung around and squinted. "Who is it Ettie? I can't see without my glasses."

"You won't believe this, Elsa-May. Sit down." When Elsa-May sat back down, Ettie said, "It's Sarah King."

"Titus's wife."

"And Nell's *schweschder*-in-law. What would she know about Jedidiah? I did say she spoke about him as though he was alive, didn't I? You didn't listen to me."

"Perhaps she's not who we were meant to meet."

When Sarah got closer, Ettie knew she was the one who'd written the note because she smiled and walked right up to them.

"Sarah, it's you we're meeting?" Elsa-May asked.

"*Jah,* it's me who wrote the note. I'm sorry I'm late. I had a visitor and had trouble getting away."

"You're here now. Have a seat." Ettie and Elsa-May moved to make room in between themselves for Sarah. "What is it you know about Jedidiah?" Ettie asked.

"It's not what I know, it's what Titus told me. He told me many years ago and has never spoken of it since, even after you came the other day asking questions. And then when that body was found and I saw how upset Nell was I couldn't keep my silence any longer."

"What is it?" Elsa-May asked.

"Titus won't be happy with me telling you this. I had to say things the other day to throw you off the track, so it would sound like I knew nothing, but then I felt so guilty."

"Go on," Ettie said.

"I don't know the full story of the thing, but I know he's alive. Jedidiah was in a hurry to get away. He told Titus he was going to live close by as an *Englischer* and he was going to melt into the crowd."

"Is that right?" Elsa-May covered her mouth in shock.

Sarah continued, "Titus bought him some clothes so he would blend in, and then Jedidiah went to a nearby town. And don't ask me where." She shrugged her shoulders. "I've racked my brains trying to remember and I can't ask Titus again, or he'll be suspicious I'm telling someone and he'll be upset."

"I thought he seemed a little uptight when we asked him questions," Ettie said.

"I think he thought I was going to say something when you were there the other day."

"He would've been nervous. Undoubtedly." Elsa-May nodded.

"Jedidiah left and I don't know why. This is all true."

"Does Titus know exactly where he is?" Elsa-May asked.

Sarah turned to Elsa-May. "If he has his address, he didn't tell me. And you can't ask him anything, or he'll know I told you this much."

Elsa-May leaned over and patted her hand. *"Denke* for telling us, Sarah. This makes things a lot easier for us now that we know he's still out there somewhere. And, hopefully he still is out there somewhere."

"Denke for not asking Titus questions again. It makes me so upset when he gets cranky with me. I try to be a *gut fraa."*

Ettie said, "I'm sure you do, but many other people are involved in this, not just Titus. You've done a good thing, Sarah."

"What are you going to do now?" Sarah asked.

Elsa-May said, "We're going to try to find him."

She sprang to her feet. "I have to get back before Titus notices I'm missing."

"Denke, Sarah."

"Jah," Ettie added, "this saves us a lot of time and worry."

Sarah leaned down and gave each lady a quick hug before she left. The two ladies sat and watched her walk away until she disappeared around a curve at the other end of the park.

Elsa-May gave a deep sigh and faced Ettie. "What do you think of that?"

"We thought he might be alive. How do we even begin to find him?"

"We can't. Not on our own."

Ettie stroked her chin. "You're right. We'll have to tell Detective Kelly and he can do some digging. He said people always leave a trace and with all the modern technology at his fingertips, he'd do a far better job than we can."

"*Nee,* he'll talk to Titus. We can't let that happen, or Sarah will not forgive us. And Titus would make Sarah's life miserable."

Ettie put a finger in the air. "But, if he's still out there somewhere he could have heard about the body having been found. If you were Jedidiah and you heard about the body found at Rose Cottage, what would you do?"

"That would depend on why I chose to leave. Did he accidently or deliberately kill this man, and was that why he left? If we're totally honest with ourselves, we must know that one or the other of those reasons is the thing that made him leave."

"Hmm, it's a hard one."

"Is he still living nearby, or has he moved away? He could have a whole other life now. He could have married and had a family."

Ettie added, "He could even have died."

"That's true. If he's alive and never married, he might try to contact Nell if he's heard about Abraham's death." Elsa-May sighed. "There are so many possibilities."

"We could tell Kelly we've found out he's living nearby as an *Englischer.*" Ettie pushed her lips together, thinking and wondering what to do. She continued, "Then he'll question us about how we found out. We'll have to speak with Titus again. He's the only one who knows anything."

"We can't! We can't possibly. Sarah would never forgive us. And we promised." Elsa-May shook her head so vigorously that her bottom lip wobbled.

"Hmm. There must be a way around this."

"The only thing we can do is give Kelly the information and not tell him how we found out. We can refuse to tell him, and that's not lying."

"I suppose you're right." Ettie looked around the park. They seldom had time these days to relax in a place such as this. "It would be so lovely to bring sandwiches here one day and feed the ducks the leftovers. Why don't we ever do anything like that?"

"Because we've got too much to do." Elsa-May stood and as she did so, she put her hand under Ettie's arm to lift her to her feet. "Let's tell Kelly what we know."

"I'm going to come back here when we find Jedidiah and this whole thing is over. I'm going to sit down by myself even if you don't come with me."

"Alright. I'll come with you. I'll even make the sandwiches if you put a smile on your face."

Ettie smiled even though she didn't want to.

"That's the way." Elsa-May started walking with her hand now looped through Ettie's, and Ettie had no choice but to place one foot after the other.

CHAPTER 18

THE POLICE STATION was a few blocks away from the park and just as Ettie and Elsa-May were on the sidewalk outside, Kelly's car drew alongside them. He beeped the horn, and Elsa-May pulled on Ettie's sleeve. "It's Kelly."

They hurried over to him.

"Are you here to see me?" he asked from the driver's seat.

"Yes, we wanted to tell you that there is a rumor— "

Elsa-May cut across Ettie, "It's a little

more than a rumor. We have reason to believe that Jedidiah has been living as an *Englischer* close by. Well, he was when he first left."

"We've just put out an APB on Jedidiah Shoneberger. If you have any information, you must tell me now."

Ettie gasped. "Are you going to arrest him?"

"He's wanted for questioning regarding the murder of Arnold Salisbury."

"You found out the man was definitely murdered?" He hadn't told them anything about that before.

"His skull was crushed and it wasn't from a fall. Someone hit him with a hard blunt object. The medical examiner said it was most likely a hammer. We know that the two men had a falling out." He stared at both of them intently. "Nothing else to say?"

"We can't help more than that," Ettie said.

Elsa-May added, "That's all we know."

He gave them a sharp nod and the car zoomed away.

"That wasn't too hard, Ettie."

"If Jedidiah didn't kill that man, who did?"

Ettie sighed. "That's the question."

"We've had a big day already and I need to sit and rest these weary bones."

"I wouldn't mind filling my tank again."

Elsa-May chuckled. "I know just the place for that."

"*Jah*, but no more chocolate cake."

Elsa-May frowned. "Halves?"

"*Nee*, it's far too rich for me. I prefer something not so sickly-sweet."

"We'll find something we both like and we'll go halves. Happy?"

Ettie nodded and together they walked up the road to what had become their favorite café.

. . .

As THEY SAT at a quiet table with their hot tea, waiting for their carrot cake with cream cheese frosting, Ettie asked, "What do we know about the dead man?"

"He wanted to buy back Rose Cottage."

"And?"

Elsa-May took a sip of the hot tea and Ettie was pleased she didn't make that dreadful slurping sound that she often made when she was at home. Elsa-May finally said, "Salisbury was trying to sell his land to the corporation."

"Hmm. The corporation we know nothing about. Perhaps we should look into that?"

Elsa-May nodded and then there it was—the slurp.

"*Ach,* Elsa-May, do you have to always do that?" Ettie hissed.

Elsa-May set the cup carefully on the saucer and then looked up at Ettie. "What?"

Ettie shook her head in disgust. "Forget it."

The waitress brought their cake to the table.

"Thank you," When the waitress left, Ettie picked up a knife and went to divide it in two, but Elsa-May got there before her.

"Was I drinking too noisy again?"

"Just a little."

"We're getting off the track. You've got to focus, Ettie. You were talking about the corporation."

"We've got to find out more about them."

Elsa-May carefully cut the cake into two pieces and put half onto her saucer and passed the plate to Ettie. *"Jah,* the corporation. Why didn't they just buy the land from Jedidiah if it meant so much."

"It doesn't work like that. Maybe they didn't even know that man didn't still own the cottage. It takes a while for the paperwork to go through at the land titles office, doesn't it?"

Elsa-May shrugged. "Don't know."

"Also, what happened to all that man's land after his death?"

"Disappearance, not death," Elsa-May corrected.

"He's officially dead now, but what happens to someone's property when they've disappeared for that long? How long is it before the family could have him declared 'presumed dead' or whatever the term is?" Ettie cut into her cake with a fork and broke off a piece. "Hmm. How do we find out all of this? We need to know what happened to his land. Was it sold when it passed into the hands of his benefactors? Or did it pass on to them? Or, maybe it just stayed as is for all those years." She popped the bite of cake into her mouth. It wasn't as nice as the lemon cake, but it was a good compromise.

"We should find that out. And, we

could've asked Kelly if he hadn't been in such a hurry."

Ettie swallowed her mouthful. "Let's go and visit Edgar again."

"Why him?"

"Jedidiah confided in him, that's why."

"He might give us a clue, I suppose." Elsa-May stared at her half of the cake.

"Try some."

"It's not chocolate."

"It's not bad. In fact, it's quite good. Try it. It's better for you."

Elsa-May muttered, "That's why I know it's not going to taste as good."

Ettie chuckled.

CHAPTER 19

ETTIE AND ELSA-MAY found Edgar in the games room again. His face lit up when he saw them and he looked even more pleased when Elsa-May held up the paper bag of candy. He knew what was inside. Fortunately, Ettie had remembered the licorice. They'd stopped at a candy store on the way.

"Thank you, ladies. You came again."

"We did and we brought licorice."

"Ah, thank you." He reached out for the bag and Elsa-May handed it to him.

He was sitting with the same man as the first time they'd visited, playing chess. Doug smiled at them again and after he nodded, he wheeled himself away. The ladies pulled up chairs and sat down with Edgar.

He pulled open the bag and popped a piece of licorice into his mouth, closed his eyes and savored it. When he opened his eyes, he held the bag toward them. "Want some?"

"No, thank you. We've just eaten."

He twisted the top of the bag and placed it in his lap. "It's nice to see you both again. Have you found Jedidiah yet?"

Ettie shook her head. "No, we haven't."

"I read in the paper that they found the remains of a body at Rose Cottage."

"Do you know who it was?" Ettie asked.

He rubbed his stubbly chin. "Should I?"

Elsa-May leaned over to him. "Arnold Salisbury. He's the man who was trying to buy back Rose Cottage."

His eyes widened. "Oh. That was his name."

"He disappeared around the same time as Jedidiah."

"Yes," Elsa-May said, "and now the police are looking for Jedidiah to question him."

"You say the man had been murdered?"

"We didn't say so, but he was. With a hammer," Elsa-May said.

Edgar looked down and shook his head. "It doesn't look good for Jedidiah."

"No, it doesn't."

"I'm sure he didn't do it. He wasn't capable. What can I help you with?"

"Well, we came to ask you if you know anything about the corporation who tried to buy that land? We've been told it was a big company. Do you know anything about it? Or, do you know the names of any companies that were buying up land back then?"

He shook his head. "It was a long time ago."

"Can you give it some thought? It's really important."

"I'll give it some thought and when you visit me again, I'll tell you if I've remembered anything."

Ettie leaned forward. "Elsa-May meant can you try to remember now."

He closed his eyes for a couple of moments and then opened them. "No, nothing's there. I can't help you."

Elsa-May and Ettie exchanged glances.

Ettie tried something else. "Did you know any of Jedidiah's friends? He had Nell's brother helping him fix the cottage and he had other helpers there from time to time."

"No, they were all the same to me. I remember a young lad helping out."

"That would've been Titus, Nell's brother."

"Yes, that was his name. Then there were a couple of other men there, but I can't tell you anything about them. I don't remember their names and I might never have been introduced to them. It's all hazy. I helped him at the house for a couple of days and that was that."

"Do you remember the dates?"

He chuckled. "I'd have no way of knowing that. It was all too long ago. I never kept a diary and my work notes are all thrown away years ago when I closed the business down."

"Well, thank you for your help."

"It was a pleasure." He lifted the bag out of his lap. "Thank you for this. I can't get out to get any. I can get out, but I can't walk around much. It's too much effort."

Elsa-May pushed herself to her feet. "You're welcome."

"Goodbye and thank you once again," Ettie said. Then she asked, "Do you think someone was there to help him?"

"No."

"Do you know where he might be living now? Someone told us he moved to a nearby town."

"I'm sorry, I can't help you, ladies. All I know is what I know. I can't say what I don't know."

"We wouldn't want you to do that," Elsa-May said with amusement.

"Now, how about a game of chess?"

Elsa-May moved closer to him and then crouched down in front of him. "Edgar, if you had to make a wild guess where Jedidiah would've gone, where would you say?"

He was quiet for a moment, and then said, "I'm sorry, I can't help you. I saw that the bully's funeral is on Monday. I saw it in the paper."

They looked at Edgar in surprise. "The bully?" Ettie asked.

"The man who was trying to buy Rose Cottage back."

"Ah, Arnold Salisbury."

"They found him dead in the garden. I read it in the paper today. The funeral is next week. I saw that too. It was in a different part of the paper. I always read the funeral notices to see if I know anyone who's dead."

When they first talked with him he hadn't mentioned having read it in the paper. That confirmed to Ettie that he wasn't in his right mind. Kelly had thought he was. "Yes, we heard that. Do you think Jedidiah had anything to do with it?"

"Jedidiah who?"

"Never mind," Ettie said. "Enjoy your licorice. We should go, Elsa-May."

As they were walking away, he called after them, "I told him he needed to stand up to that bully and order him off the property, but he was too gentle." His voice reverberated around the room and everyone looked over at him.

On their way down the front ramp of the building, Ettie said, "Well, we tried."

"It was a waste of time."

"Now, we should go back and talk with Nell. Perhaps she holds a clue without realizing it."

Elsa-May nodded in agreement.

CHAPTER 20

GLORIA, Nell's granddaughter, opened the door of Rose Cottage.

"Is your grandmother home?" Elsa-May asked sweetly. It was a tone that Ettie didn't often hear from her sister.

"*Jah*, come in."

They followed Gloria into the living room where Nell sat reading a newspaper.

"I'm glad it's you two come to visit me again. Sit down." Nell patted the couch next to her. "Gloria, would you be a dear and make us some hot tea?"

"Of course."

When Gloria walked out of the room, Nell said, "She's been such a comfort. I don't know what I'd do without her. She's been staying here with me and cheering me up. I feel like I've been living in a nightmare that I can't wake up from. A total nightmare. It's such an awful feeling that the man was buried right by the house. And it can't have been an accidental death because he was buried. Someone covered him up. He must've been killed."

It still hadn't occurred to Nell that everything pointed to Jedidiah being the guilty party. Ettie was running out of things to say to comfort her.

Elsa-May said, "They're having a funeral for Arnold Salisbury this upcoming Monday."

"I must pay my respects. Someone said his wife died five years after his disappearance. The poor woman. The stress of it all probably killed her. I know what it's like living with not knowing what's happened to a person. I would like to go to his funeral. Do you know when it is?"

"*Nee,* not exactly," Ettie said, "but we'll find out."

"Could you?"

Ettie nodded, not quite sure how she'd find out. Surely there would be a notice in the local newspapers, as that was how Edgar learned of it.

"Would you both go with me?"

Ettie smiled and reached out and held Nell's hand. "Of course we'll go with you, won't we, Elsa-May?"

Elsa-May nodded. "If that's what you want, we'll go with you."

Gloria came in with a tray of tea items and set them down on a table and then poured each lady a cup of tea.

"I don't know why that Arnold man even bought Rose Cottage in the first place. It just lay abandoned for years. No one lived here. There was so much work to do when we got it. You should've seen it."

"Abraham did a lot of work to it over the years," Elsa-May commented. "The other people probably just had it as an investment it seems. Maybe just for the value of the plot of land."

"Abraham loved the place as much as I did. We had a happy life, and now the memories of that will fade just as the memories of Jedidiah faded into the background. It was another lifetime—a different lifetime." She looked at Ettie. "I'm rambling. It's something that's hard to explain."

"You don't have to explain anything."

"Since it was well known that the two men, Jedidiah and Salisbury were at loggerheads over Rose cottage, do you think the family will be a little unwelcoming toward us at his funeral?" Elsa-May asked.

"I don't see why they would be. Jedidiah

gave it to me and I lived in it with Abraham. It was almost as though Jedidiah was a previous owner and I was the next one. I didn't even know them, so how would they be upset with me?"

Ettie gulped and looked at Elsa-May. She sure hoped Nell was right because she didn't want to upset the family at the funeral. Elsa-May was nodding at what Nell said, as though she was making perfect sense, but what if they knew Jedidiah was a suspect and they knew Nell was once promised to marry him? It might look to them like Nell was a co-conspirator.

After their tea, and a lot more conversation about days gone by, Ettie and Elsa-May finally walked out of Nell's house. Nell had Gloria hitch the buggy to take them home.

They had only gone two steps toward the waiting buggy when Nell called after them, "Don't forget to tell me when the funeral is. I'll have John drive us there if it's not too far."

"*Jah,* I'll let you know," Ettie said.

Elsa-May stage-whispered, "We avoided one funeral, and now we're roped into going to another one. *Gott* is showing His sense of humor."

Ettie dug Elsa-May in the ribs. "Shh. Gloria might hear you."

Elsa-May chuckled.

ETTIE FOUND out that Arnold Salisbury's funeral was to be held in a chapel at the main building of the Garden Lawn Cemetery. The newspaper announcement had stated that the funeral was to be non-denominational.

Since it was a little too far to go by buggy, the three ladies traveled by taxi. All the way there, Ettie's heart pounded. She was fervently hoping they weren't making a big mistake by going.

They stepped out of the taxi and Ettie

looked at the plain square building. It reminded her of Edgar's retirement home. There were two men in dark suits talking outside, and a couple of cars were pulling into the parking lot.

"Not many people are here yet," Nell whispered.

"They might all be inside," Ettie said then she jumped when Elsa-May poked her in the ribs. "I wish you wouldn't do that, Elsa-May!"

"Come on. We'll be late if you don't move along."

"You go ahead. I'll be right behind you." When Ettie hung back, Elsa-May strode ahead.

Ettie and Nell followed Elsa-May through the door. They followed a sign directing mourners to the chapel, went in, and took seats in the back row. Ettie counted twenty-five people including a grim-looking man sitting up at the front.

Ettie whispered to Nell, who was sitting in the middle, "That must be the fellow handling the funeral service. The non-denominational person."

"It looks like it."

Elsa-May leaned across Nell, and looked directly at Ettie. "Shhh."

Ettie stifled a giggle. Her older sister looked so much like their mother when she pulled that stern face.

The dark shiny coffin was on one side of the room, and a microphone on a stand took center stage. Sitting in the front rows were a few middle-aged couples. Ettie guessed they were Arnold Salisbury's children and their spouses.

"Still not many people here," Nell whispered to Ettie.

Ettie could only nod in agreement, not daring to upset Elsa-May. They hadn't been thrown out yet, but still, Ettie felt out of place and couldn't help wondering if someone was going to be asking them to leave.

A song was played over the loudspeaker. Ettie caught a few words about life, but most of the words were mumbled. It was modern music and Ettie wasn't used to it. When the song ended, a man got up to speak. Ettie soon learned he was the oldest son.

Nell leaned over, and whispered to Elsa-May, "He looks like a nice person."

"He does."

Ettie had a hard time not leaning across to shush her sister.

When the service was over, the son who had spoken approached them.

"Hello. I'm Frank Salisbury. Can I ask how you knew my father?"

"My name is Nell Graber and I live in Rose Cottage. These are my friends, Elsa-May Lutz and Ettie Smith."

His face lit up with a smile. "I loved to play in that old place when I was a kid. I like what you've done with it. I've driven by it over the years. Were you a friend of my father or my mother?"

Ettie was immediately relieved. He knew nothing of the past tension between his father and Jedidiah.

"No, I wasn't, but I wanted to come anyway because of the connection, and you are sort of my neighbors."

"Do you still live in the area?" Elsa-May asked.

"After my mother passed away, my father was still missing, so my brothers and I were sent to live with our grandparents in California."

Nell said, "You would've been young when your mother died."

"I was."

"Do you mind me asking what happened to your father's land?" Nell asked.

"The land adjoining your place?"

"Yes."

"I guess it will be divided amongst the three of us boys. Did you have some interest in buying some of it?"

"Oh, no. I was just curious."

"I know my father was giving someone grief over Rose Cottage. He bought and sold properties all the time but I remember him telling me his biggest mistake was selling Rose Cottage too quickly. I was only a kid, but I remember him telling me he was trying to get it back because it was more valuable than he knew when he sold it."

"I was told that it led to a road that would be beneficial to someone else who wanted to buy that and some other land from your father."

"I believe so. Do you want to sell it now?" he asked Nell with a twinkle in his eye.

"Never. I'd never sell."

He smiled as though he didn't have a care if she sold or not.

Ettie hoped he wouldn't become like his

father if the land still held that same value. Ettie asked, "Would you happen to know the name of the company that wanted to buy the land back then?"

He looked thoughtfully at Ettie and slowly shook his head. "No. I don't remember, and I was probably never told. I was just a kid back then." He turned to face Nell. "It's nice you found a place you feel so strongly about."

"I've always liked the place," said Nell. "You should've seen it when I was a child. It was beautiful and the roses were huge and red, some of them so dark they were nearly black. I used to stop by there with a particular friend of mine. Then it lay vacant and quickly fell into ruin."

Ettie held her breath hoping she wouldn't mention Jedidiah's name. Thankfully, it appeared Frank was growing bored talking to three old ladies, because his eyes were now wandering over the crowd.

"Oh, forgive us. We're keeping all your attention away from other people. I'm sure there are many who'd need to speak with you," Ettie said.

His lips turned upward into a broad smile. "There are people here I haven't seen for years. It was nice to talk to you ladies. We have refreshments in the adjoining room if you'd like to stay on. The burial is later today, and that's family only."

Nell shook her head. "I don't think we'll stay, but thank you."

He nodded. "It was nice to meet you all." Then he turned away.

When he was out of hearing range, Nell said, "I hope that's all right with the both of you that we don't stay?"

"Jah, of course." Ettie wanted to get away from the place as soon as she could, and she knew Elsa-May felt the same.

CHAPTER 21

EARLY THE NEXT MORNING, Ettie sat at the kitchen table eating oatmeal soaked in warm milk with honey drizzled over the top.

Elsa-May staggered into the kitchen tying her dressing gown while Snowy trotted happily alongside her. "What are you so thoughtful about?"

"We're going to have a dinner here and tell everyone that Arnold Salisbury's murderer will be revealed."

"What?"

"You heard me."

"Do you know who killed him?"

Ettie shook her head and kept eating.

"Then it's a dumb idea, and you don't like having people here."

"That's not true. It's just that the place is so small it doesn't lend itself to events, or big dinners."

Elsa-May asked, "Who's coming?"

"Everyone we've talked to about Jedidiah."

"To flush someone out?"

Ettie nodded. "Possibly."

"Oh, Ettie. Anyone could've killed that man for all we know. A man like that would've made many enemies along the way. We still haven't found out about that company."

Ettie grunted. "It doesn't matter about that anymore. Not now that we know Jedidiah is still alive. That would've been important if Jedidiah had been found dead, or if it were his body found at Rose Cottage."

"No need to be snippy with me."

"Jedidiah was living at Rose Cottage at the time, while he was fixing the place. He disappeared for a reason. Either he killed the man, or ...."

"How do you know he's not dead? I mean, you can't believe everything people tell you."

"Titus wouldn't have lied to Sarah."

"But—"

"Don't say another thing, Elsa-May. You're throwing me off my train of thought and it's too early in the morning for chatter. It's a possibility he might have died over the past few years, but if he hasn't, he's still out there somewhere."

"Hmm, someone's in a mood," she said quietly to Snowy.

"We're going to invite Edgar. We'll visit him today and if he agrees to come, we'll arrange for them to send him here in a taxi on that night."

"Edgar?"

"Jah." Ettie gave a sharp nod of her head.

"Okay. I'm not arguing now that I see you're in this mood."

Ettie smiled to herself and continued to eat her breakfast while planning out the dinner. Elsa-May's talk was just background noise now.

THEY WERE SHOWN into the dayroom where Edgar was sitting in the sun and reading the paper.

"Hello, Edgar."

He put the paper down when he saw them and a huge smiled beamed across his face. "Ah, I hoped you'd be back. Sit down."

After they sat, Ettie said, "I'm having a few people over for dinner on Thursday night and Elsa-May and I were wondering if you'd like to come."

"I sure would. Anything to get out of this place." He looked down at their hands. "Did you bring any—"

"No, we forgot. How about we have some on Thursday night for you?"

He smiled and nodded. "I like the sound of that. I've still got some left. I have a small piece every day. It's something to look forward to at night."

Ettie looked around the dayroom. It was early and not many residents were there. Ettie could hold back no longer. She moved her chair closer to Edgar, and said, "Between the three of us, if you admit what you did, then Jedidiah can come out of hiding. He's protecting you by remaining silent, isn't he?"

He stared at her for a moment before he spoke. "Look, lady, it was purely self-defence."

Elsa-May gasped. "You did it?"

"He had a gun."

"Tell us what happened," Ettie said.

"He pointed a gun at Jedidiah. I distracted him with a hammer. Was he going to shoot? I wasn't about to wait around and find out. Jedidiah was my friend. In my experience, if someone points a gun at someone they aint muckin' about."

Ettie said, "Don't you see? If we find him, and he backs up your story you won't go to jail."

He scoffed. "We'll both go to jail."

"I don't think so." Ettie shook her head.

"Hey, I've been in jail more times than I can count on my fingers. I'd have to start using my toes. They won't believe me, and what makes you think they'll believe Jedidiah? They'll think we both cooked this thing up together."

Ettie frowned and wondered if he was right. Because he'd been in and out of jail, would anyone believe him? And, by covering up the body for so long, they'd added another crime to the mix. "I don't know what will happen, but won't you feel better with this all being out in the open after all this time?"

He frowned, gritted his teeth, and said, "Take a look around."

Ettie and Elsa-May looked around the room.

"I can do what I like 'round here. I can go out for the day and come back to a place I call home. Have you ever been inside a prison?"

"Only to visit people," Ettie said.

"The food's inedible, the people hostile, the guards egomaniacs, and every ounce of humanity is stripped away. Do you think I want to spend the rest of my days being told what to do every second?" He held up his hands. "What's done is done. Leave things alone. You wouldn't want to see me go to prison, would you?"

"No, we wouldn't." Elsa-May said.

"Then keep quiet." He put his finger to his mouth. "Mum's the word."

ETTIE AND ELSA-MAY LEFT, not knowing what to do.

"Ettie, how did you know?"

"I guessed he was lying about something because he was just pretending to have lost his mind. I didn't believe it. He must have acted perfectly normal around Kelly because Kelly said he was in his right mind, or something like that. It just seemed odd he was okay with us one minute and then put on that act the next minute."

"I see. Why didn't you share that with me?"

Ettie frowned at her sister. "What?"

"What you thought."

"I only thought about it just when I said it. I didn't come here thinking that."

"Oh. You weren't thinking that over breakfast?"

"*Nee.* Anyway, he's right, Elsa-May. In a perfect world he'd be believed, but the world's not perfect. Justice is not always served."

Elsa-May huffed impatiently. "Are you saying we just leave things as they are?"

"*Jah,* maybe that's what we have to do. Even Kelly wouldn't be able to guarantee the outcome."

"What if things aren't what he said? What if he knows Jedidiah would tell us a different story and that's why he doesn't want us to find him?"

"Hmm, good thinking. Go back and make sure he's coming to the dinner," Ettie said.

Elsa-May's eyebrows rose. "Me?"

"*Jah,* he likes you better. He keeps smiling at you."

"Um, I don't think he's looking at me. I think he's slightly cross-eyed."

"Just do it, would you?"

Elsa-May heaved a sigh. "Okay, but I don't think it's nice if he's going to be ambushed."

"Just trust me for once. We'll tell everyone that the murderer will be revealed at our place at the dinner. Just don't tell Edgar that. We'll have Detective Kelly there, too."

Elsa-May's shoulders hunched over. "Are you certain about that?"

"Trust me."

Elsa-May rolled her eyes and went back to talk with Edgar.

CHAPTER 22

EVERYONE THEY'D INVITED to the dinner was there. Ettie and Elsa-May's small house was bursting at the seams. They'd moved the table out of the kitchen and everyone was eating the finger foods they'd prepared.

Ettie was getting nervous, and she hoped that everything would play out as it had in her head.

No one else noticed another knock on the door, but Ettie knew everyone she'd invited was there. Even Edgar Upton, who was being entertained by one of Nell's stories about the old days. Was it Jedidiah at the door? No one else was expected. Ettie opened the door, wondering for an instant if it would be Greville asking her to keep the noise down. She opened the door to see it wasn't Greville. It was his wife.

"Is everything all right, Ettie? We saw a lot of people here and we never usually see so many people at your house."

"We've got visitors." Ettie was annoyed with the woman. Their new neighbors had only lived there for a few short weeks, so why would they think they knew what was normal? She'd already opened her mail, and now she was nosey about their guests. "In fact, we often have many people here."

Stacey tried to look over Ettie's shoulder, but Ettie moved to block her view. Was the woman looking for an invitation? "All's fine here," Ettie fixed a smile on her face.

"That's good. I'll see you again."

She turned and headed down the steps.

"Oh, and don't worry about the mail. I'll call the mail delivery people and ask them to put our mail fully in our box next time."

"Very well."

Ettie closed the door, pining for the good neighbor who used to live beside them. Stacey wasn't nasty like her husband, but she sure was becoming annoying. No sooner had Ettie taken a step from the door than another knock sounded. She opened the door ready to answer another silly question from Stacey, but it was someone else. Ettie's jaw fell open as she looked into a familiar but much older face than the one she'd remembered. "Jedidiah Shoneberger."

"Ettie Smith."

"You got my invitation?" Ettie had a hunch that if Titus knew, it wouldn't be long before Jedidiah found out. It confirmed to Ettie that her suspicion had been right; Titus had kept in touch with him.

"Is that what it was?"

"In a roundabout way."

"I heard a whisper this was to be an important night." He leaned forward. "Is Nell here?"

"Jah."

"Can you send her out here, so I can have a word with her before I come inside?"

Ettie nodded and pulled the door closed, then looked around for Nell. Nell had moved from Edgar to Detective Kelly. This wasn't going to be easy, since Kelly and the rest of the police force were looking for Jedidiah. "Excuse me, Nell, can I have a word with you in the kitchen?"

"Okay." She turned to Kelly. "I won't forget where I'm up to."

Once they were in the kitchen, Ettie whispered, "Jedidiah is here, and—" Ettie stopped when Jennifer walked into the kitchen. Now things were really bad. Ettie hoped Nell could keep silent or Jennifer could ruin everything.

Nell's fingers flew to her mouth. "He's here?"

"Who's here?"

Ettie stepped forward. "Snowy, Elsa-May's little dog. He's here, but he's asleep in Elsa-May's room."

Jennifer looked at Nell. "Why would you be excited about a dog?"

"He's so cute. Can I see him, Ettie."

"Okay, but we must open the door and get in before he gets out. He'll run around and be a nuisance if he does. Would you like to see him too, Jennifer?"

Jennifer crossed her arms over her chest. "*Nee.*"

Jennifer wasn't going anywhere, so Ettie had to slip into Elsa-May's bedroom with Nell to pretend they were looking at the dog.

Once they were in the room, Nell said, "He's here?"

"*Jah.* He's outside. He's going to come in, but he's asking to speak with you first."

Nell put her fingers to her lips. "How am I going to do that without Jennifer seeing me go outside? She'll follow me."

Ettie sighed. "You'll have to go out the window, and then down the side of the house and around to the front. There's the side gate to go through, but it's not locked."

"Oh! Well, if that's the only way. *Denke,* Ettie."

"Kelly wants to talk with him and if you want to see him first, you must slip out without being seen." Ettie repeated, "Jedidiah wants to see you before he comes in. Got it?"

She nodded and blew out a deep breath. "Is he okay?"

"He looks okay. Now go, see for yourself." Ettie pushed up the window while Nell bunched up her dress into her hands. When she was gone, Ettie closed the window. Now she was stuck in the bedroom. She opened the door just slightly and saw Jennifer leaning against the door of the kitchen. Ettie closed the door again and sat on the bed beside a sleeping Snowy.

Snowy stirred and lifted his head. "We're both trapped in here, Snowy. I could see in Nell's eyes she still loves Jedidiah. I hope they have a happy ending after all they've been through." Ettie sighed. "I hope Jedidiah didn't do anything silly."

Snowy inched forward and rested his head on Ettie's lap and Ettie stroked his fur. He went back to sleep, and she felt some of the stress seep from her body.

CHAPTER 23

EVEN WITH HER LARGE FRAME, Nell didn't have trouble getting herself out that window. When her apron caught on the corner, she didn't care whether it might tear. She yanked at that apron until she heard a rip as it came free. Nothing was going to keep her from Jedidiah. She pushed open the side gate Ettie had told her about and then she found herself at the front of the house. There he was, by the front gate.

"Jedidiah." Nell ran to him and her hands immediately went to his face. He was real and very much alive. By the dim lighting, she could see that his once fresh and handsome face was now weathered. Deep lines marred his brow and the corners of his eyes.

He took hold of her hands and held them while staring into her eyes. "I've missed you so much." He pulled her to him and held her tight.

He was older, and like her, he'd gotten a little wider, but he was still her Jedidiah. She stepped out of the embrace. "Why did you leave? Where have you been?"

"I don't know where to start. It's a long story. I never stopped thinking about you. I thought about you nearly every second of every day. You were in my heart and still are."

A tear trickled down her cheek and she didn't want to move her hand from his to wipe it away. "Why did you leave?"

"You'll soon find out. I didn't know if you knew already."

"*Nee,* I know nothing. They found that man, Salisbury, who used to own the cottage."

"You must trust me, Nell."

"Are you going to leave me again?"

He wiped the tears from her face. Then he pulled her into him again. In his arms, nothing had changed; it was as it was back then, and she knew they belonged together.

"Just trust me," he whispered in her ear.

"I'll try." She hoped he had a good reason for having left her. There was nothing she could think of that would make up for putting her through the pain she'd endured, but she was prepared to listen to what he had to say.

"I'll tell you everything soon. Right now, I need to go in and face something I should've faced many years ago." He moved back a little and wiped away more of her tears. He smiled at her. "Are you ready to come inside?"

She moved closer and put her arms around him. "I can't believe you're alive. I thought you were dead all these years. That's the only thing that made sense. I would never have left you—never."

"I'm sorry, Nell. From the bottom of my heart, I'm sorry. I'll spend the rest of my life making it up to you. I'll do whatever you want. If you want me to leave you alone I will. If you want me to chop my arm off I'll do it. I'll do—"

Nell's body trembled. "Stop."

"I'm serious, Nell. I want you to be happy and I want to make up for leaving you."

"Go and do what you have to do and we'll go from there." She felt much better now that he knew how much he'd hurt her. Now that he was there and very much alive, she never wanted to let him go.

He took a deep breath. "I'll go in."

"And I'll be right beside you."

He nodded, and gave her a smile.

ETTIE TOOK another peep into the room. It wouldn't be long before someone came looking for her. It felt like twenty minutes had gone by and Ettie became worried. Had Jedidiah and Nell run away together?

Then the door opened and Jedidiah walked through the door with Nell right by him. Ettie slipped through the bedroom door and closed it behind her. She looked at Detective Kelly and then realized he had no idea who Jedidiah was by sight. As was customary among the Amish, there had never been any photograph taken of him.

But then Ettie noticed Jedidiah and Edgar's eyes locked together. Ettie knew she had to do something fast.

Ettie clapped her hands and stood in the middle of the room. "Jedidiah Shoneberger is here." Everyone gasped and stared at him. "He came here to tell us about the mystery of why he left so suddenly and what really happened to Arnold Salisbury."

Kelly jumped to his feet and then stopped in his tracks when Edgar called out, "It's over, Jedidiah. I can no longer keep quiet." All eyes were on Edgar and he continued, "It was selfish of me to keep quiet for so long. Jedidiah is innocent and he took off to keep my secret."

"And what secret was that?" Detective Kelly grunted.

"Don't say anything else," Titus said to Edgar.

Ettie gulped. Did she get it all wrong?

Titus went on, saying, "It was my fault. Salisbury came to the house when I was working there and asked me what it would take to make Jedidiah sell. I told him nothing would." Everyone stared at Titus waiting for him to continue.

Eventually, Nell asked, "What do you mean, Titus? Why was it your fault?"

"Sit down, Titus. Keep your mouth shut. I'm an old man. It doesn't matter so much. You've got a family."

"I can't keep quiet. I need to unburden my soul. The next day, Salisbury came looking for Jedidiah again. I was there with Jedidiah, so was Moses, and also Edgar."

Everyone looked at Moses and he looked down at the floorboards.

Titus continued, "I told Salisbury to stay away. That Jedidiah wouldn't sell no matter what."

"It was my fault," Moses said. "I angered Salisbury by something I said. I told him he would never amount to anything. I taunted him for selling the key to his potential fortune— Rose Cottage. I must've hit a nerve; he pulled out a gun …"

Jedidiah said, "He pointed it at Moses and I thought he'd shoot. I grabbed the nearest thing I could. It was an instinctive thing. I did not remember my commandments."

"Don't lie for me, Jedidiah. It was the other way around." Edgar turned to Kelly. "You know the Amish wouldn't raise a hand to anyone."

Kelly nodded. "What happened?"

"Jedidiah struck him in the back of the legs with the wood in his hands. When Salisbury was down, he twisted and pointed the gun at Jedidiah. I grabbed a hammer and struck him on the head. I knew he'd shoot. And, that's how it happened. Jedidiah knew I'd go to jail and he was trying to protect me."

"So, what I'm hearing is self-defence." The detective looked up at Jedidiah. "Why did you run?"

"I didn't mean to go for so long, just a few weeks until we could come up with a plan. When everything calmed down, I was going to come back. I didn't know someone had buried the body right at Rose Cottage. Titus told me that later. No one knew Salisbury was dead, just missing. It made sense that I stay missing too."

"Titus! You knew where he was this whole time?" Jennifer asked.

Titus kept his head down and nodded. "I'm sorry," he uttered. "It was his choice to make."

"If *Mamm* and *Dat* were alive they'd be so ashamed of you, Titus." Jennifer then glared at Nell.

"I asked him to keep quiet," Jedidiah said. "Don't blame him, Jennifer. We were all so young back then. We didn't make the best choices."

"What did Abraham know about this?" Jennifer asked.

Nell gasped at what her sister said. "He wouldn't have known a thing."

Moses said, "Abraham wasn't there and Nell is right. He didn't know any of this."

Jennifer said, "Why was he so adamant that no one disturb the rose garden?"

Titus shrugged. "I can't say."

Jennifer turned to Nell, "You said your-self he'd never let anyone work on the building."

Nell sniffed back tears.

Titus said, "I can tell you right now that Abraham didn't know a thing about any of this."

"I can't believe all these secrets were kept." Nell looked up at Jedidiah. "I can't be-lieve you left me."

"It was the last, the very last thing I wanted to do. I was left with no choice. It was the honorable thing to do. *In honor pre-ferring one another.* That's what the word says. I was putting others before my happiness. If the police came asking about Arnold, I couldn't lie, and then Edgar, who'd been good enough to give me so much work, would've gone to jail for life."

"Or worse, with my record," Edgar called out.

"Jedidiah, did their happiness mean more than mine? You also sacrificed mine."

He sighed. "I know how you must be feeling and it's torn me apart over the years. That was wrong of me. I didn't think it would turn out the way it did. I never meant to be gone for so long. The longer I was gone the harder it became to return. Then I heard you'd become close to Abraham. Then I knew I could never come back."

Elsa-May said, "I can see how you felt, Jedidiah. Any way you turned or any decision you made was going to hurt someone."

He nodded. "The best thing I could do was to continue along the path I'd chosen."

Abraham's brother, Simon, jumped to his feet. "I've had enough for one night. *Denke*, Ettie." He nodded his head to Elsa-May instead of saying goodbye.

Before Ettie reached the front door to open it, he'd done it himself and was halfway down the porch steps. "Simon."

He turned around. *"Jah."*

"Why are you upset?"

"My *bruder* has just been buried. She couldn't even wait." He turned and walked away.

Ettie could see his point of view, but Ettie knew that Nell also had a deep love for Abraham. Nell was an innocent victim in this conspiracy. There were no easy answers for her, either.

She closed the door and walked back inside to hear Kelly say, "I'll need statements from the four of you." He pointed to Edgar, Moses, Titus, and Jedidiah.

Almost everyone had now left the dinner gathering, except for Detective Kelly and the four men he wanted to question. And Nell was still there, too. She could not keep her eyes from Jedidiah. She didn't want him to leave with the detective and the three men when the other two police officers came.

"Where are you living?" she asked Jedidiah as the officers stood at the door waiting. All she wanted to do was reach out and touch him. It was still hard to believe he was there in front of her.

"Arlington."

"Oh, that's so far."

"I'm not going back there tonight. I'm going to be staying at a bed-and-breakfast not far from you. I'll come to your place tomorrow and we'll talk some more. If you want."

"*Jah,* of course I do. I'll be waiting."

"I'll be there early." He reached out and grabbed her hand until the officers hurried him along.

She sat and watched him walk out the door. Before he walked out, he had a last look over his shoulder at her, caught her eye and gave her a little wink that gave her butterflies.

"How are you feeling?" Ettie asked as she sat down beside her.

"Oh, Ettie. I'm so happy he's alive. I can scarcely believe it. I also feel sad that he was gone for so long." She rubbed her eyes. "So many things have happened. He's coming to see me tomorrow. He lives in Arlington now."

Ettie nodded. "Are you two planning a future?"

"I don't know. We only talked for a few minutes alone. I hope so. If all goes well. You don't think he'll be charged by the police, do you?"

"*Nee,*" Elsa-May said, now joining them and sitting in her usual chair. "It was the other man who wielded the hammer."

Ettie grimaced at her sister's dreadfully descriptive words. "The detective did say it was self-defence."

"It seems he's been gone for so long for no good reason. None that I can see."

"Back then, Edgar was involved in a lot of crime. They might not have believed him and the others might have gone to jail along with him. I believe he's stayed out of trouble since, and that will help him." Ettie hoped that none of them would get into trouble for concealing the body, as that was a crime in itself.

"Would you like to stay here the night, Nell?"

"*Nee,* I asked Gloria to collect me at nine thirty. What time is it now?"

Ettie looked at the clock. "It's twenty-five minutes past."

Nell looked around. "And where is Jennifer?"

Elsa-May said, "She left not long after Simon."

"Oh. She's very cross with both me and

Titus. She's probably gone to tell Sarah what happened here tonight."

WHEN NELL LEFT, Ettie and Elsa-May sat down, exhausted.

"Well, it all turned out just as you hoped."

"*Jah.*" Ettie smiled. "I hope Nell and Jedidiah get their happy ending."

"I hope so, too. They're still in love. I haven't seen a couple look at each other like that in ages."

CHAPTER 24

THAT NIGHT, Nell couldn't sleep. She'd tossed and turned as all the pain of the past years flooded back to her. Even though she was pleased he was alive, why hadn't he reached out and told her he had to leave? She might have gone with him and together they could've had a life somewhere else. There were so many things she hadn't asked him. Was he married? Had he been married? One thing she knew for certain, if he was married she'd be devastated.

When the light of the morning sun filled

Nell's room, she stretched her hands up and was glad the night was over. Today was the day she'd have all her questions answered. Then something gnawed in the pit of her stomach. What if he didn't show? What if the police had locked him up?

She pushed the negative thoughts out of her mind, changed out of her nightdress and began the process of changing into her day clothes. As she did so, it occurred to her she was no longer the slim attractive young woman Jedidiah had fallen in love with, but there was little she could do about that.

Once dressed, she headed downstairs to prepare breakfast. Her granddaughter always slept in until midmorning—a tardy habit her parents had allowed her. Still, Nell was grateful for the peace this morning, so she could think through things a little more before Jedidiah arrived. If indeed, he came like he'd said he would.

Just as the teakettle had boiled, she saw

Jedidiah walking toward the house. She turned off the flame, smoothed back her hair under her prayer *kapp,* straightened her dress and apron, and then hurried to the front door.

She opened it and he stepped inside and pulled her toward him. She held him tight and relaxed into his chest and heard his heart beating. Then she remembered her prayer the day of Abraham's funeral. She'd asked *Gott* to let her know what had happened to him and He'd answered her prayer.

She stepped back, and whispered, "I have my *grossdochder* asleep upstairs. Come through to the kitchen." They sat together at the table. "Have you eaten?"

"*Nee.*"

"Me either. I'll fix us something."

"Not yet. Nell, will you say yes once more to marrying me?"

That answered the question of whether

he was married. "I've got so many questions. I don't know who you are anymore."

"I'm the same Jedidiah you said you'd marry over forty years ago."

"A lot has happened since then. You never married?"

"*Nee.* I kept to myself. I went to a church every Sunday, but I stayed away from the Amish in case I was recognized. Edgar and I became friends long before I left. He gave me work when no one else would, and we became friends. I knew about his past. I told him about *Gott* and he was trying to get his life right. Then the dreadful thing happened."

"Oh, Jedidiah, don't you see? I could've come with you."

"I didn't know I'd be gone long. No point in ruining both our lives." He shook his head. "I couldn't have taken you away from your family. You were so close with them all."

"Jedidiah, you would've been my family if we'd married."

He nodded. "It was probably the biggest mistake of my life."

"What happened last night with the police?"

"Ah, it seems it will be okay. I'm in the clear, but the others might be in trouble for burying the body and covering up the incident."

"That's awful."

"I'm going to visit the bishop today about returning to the community."

"He'll be surprised to see you."

"He was surprised to see me yesterday."

Nell was glad to hear it. That meant he was serious about moving back. "You saw him yesterday?"

"*Jah.* And I'm going back today to talk things over further."

"You're going to move back?"

"I am. And when you're ready I'd like us to marry." He raised his hands. "I know you'll say it's too quick and maybe it is, but how much time do we have at our stage of life?"

"I've been married once, Jedidiah."

"Nell, I thought about you every day. I dreamed and prayed that one day I'd come back, but then I couldn't when you married Abraham."

"I had to move on. I had to live my life." She reached out and touched his arm. "I truly thought you were dead. That was the only reason I could think of for why you'd left me."

"I'm alive, Nell. We've each lived a separate life when we should've lived one together. Maybe this is what *Gott* planned for us. You and Abraham had a happy life, didn't you?"

"Did Titus tell you that?"

A smile twitched at the corners of his lips. *"Jah.* He did. He said you and Abraham seemed very much in love."

"We were."

"I'm happy you were blessed with finding a man like Abraham."

"I can't marry you now, Jedidiah. Now I feel hurt that you left me. I can't push those feelings aside and find the feelings I had a long time ago." She shook her head.

His shoulders slumped. "Do you mind if I move back here, at least? To this community?"

She smiled, pleased he was going to be close by. Half of her wanted to hold him and half of her wanted to hit him. "I don't mind at all."

"Titus and Sarah said I could stay with them until I get my own place."

"That's good."

"And how do you feel about living at Rose Cottage now with Arnold Salisbury having been buried so close?" He shook his head. "It never should've been that way. I had no part in that decision."

"It doesn't bother me and we can't turn

back the clock, so it's no use getting upset. It's part of the history of this old place." She looked around the room. "It could hold more mysteries for all we know."

She smiled at him and he reached forward, held her hand and she didn't pull away. "I won't pressure you, Nell, but neither will I give up on making you my *fraa* as it should've been."

Nell stared and her heart was glad. As much as she was hurt that he left, she couldn't be apart from him for too long. She'd say yes soon, but not too soon.

It was weeks later when Kelly visited Ettie and Elsa-May.

"Come in and tell us what's happening," Ettie said. They'd already heard a few things through Titus and Sarah.

He sat down. "The prosecution isn't recommending jail time. Looks like the three of them will be free, and put on probation for several years."

Elsa-May put her hand to her chest. "That's a relief. And Jedidiah?"

"He's in the clear."

"He's moved back here, you know," Ettie told him.

"Has he?"

"*Jah.*"

"Hmm, anything to do with Nell Graber?"

Elsa-May chortled. "They're getting married. I heard a whisper about it."

"We'll have to wait and see how that goes. Now, how about a cup of hot tea?"

"You have the time?" Ettie asked.

"I do."

As Elsa-May got up to make the tea and find something to eat with it, Ettie asked him, "Are things still quiet in the station? Not enough people committing crimes?"

"We're busy enough. I'm just taking a

little time out. There's always something to do."

When Ettie heard a car, she pushed herself up and looked out the window. "We'll have to find you something to do. Like do some detective work on those neighbors of ours."

Elsa-May came back into the room with a plate of sultana cake. "Oh, Ettie, will you leave the neighbors alone. You're doing enough spying on them of your own."

When Kelly laughed, Ettie frowned at Elsa-May.

Elsa-May couldn't have cared less that she'd upset Ettie, and offered Detective Kelly some cake.

He took a piece. "This looks good."

"I baked it myself. The tea won't be long. Ettie, would you like a piece?"

Ettie looked out at Greville. He was late leaving for work. What had made him late?

"Ettie!"

Ettie swivelled her head away from the window. "Yes?"

"Cake. Do you want any?"

Ettie shook her head and then sat down to talk with Detective Kelly.

No sooner had Detective Kelly left than Ettie and Elsa-May had more visitors. This time they were surprised to see Nell and Jedidiah.

Ettie allowed the visitors to sit on the couch, and she sat on a wooden chair opposite while Elsa-May sat on her usual chair.

"Would you like cake?" Elsa-May asked, lifting up the plate of leftover cake slices from Kelly's visit.

"*Nee, denke.* We've already eaten," Jedidiah said.

"And how are you getting along now that you've moved here?" Ettie asked Jedidiah.

"Better than I could've hoped." He smiled at Nell.

"We're here today to share some news with you." Nell's face beamed with excitement.

Jedidiah cleared his throat, and said, "We wanted you to be the first people to find out."

Jedidiah and Nell smiled at each other again before Nell said, "We're getting married."

Elsa-May squealed with joy and Ettie giggled. They already knew, but acted as though they knew nothing.

"That's *wunderbaar* news." Ettie didn't normally hug people, but she stood and hugged them both, and Elsa-May did the same.

When they all sat down again, Nell asked, "You don't think I'm silly?"

Jedidiah said, "Why would it be silly?"

"*Nee*, of course not," Ettie said.

"Don't you think I'm too old to be marrying again?"

"Nonsense," Elsa-May said. "*Gott* blessed you with a second chance at love. You need to receive His blessings with a willing heart."

Nell's face lit up. "*Denke,* Elsa-May. That makes me feel so much better."

"That's what I told you," Jedidiah said.

"It sounds different when Elsa-May says it."

They all laughed.

Jedidiah then cleared his throat. "I want to thank both of you for your part in getting me back here, back to my Nell."

Ettie swiped a hand through the air. "It was all part of *Gott's* plan. We didn't even know what was happening when we first started on this journey."

Nell and Jedidiah smiled at one another.

"I don't know how everyone's going to take the news," Nell said. "The bishop has approved."

"Then that's all you need be concerned about. You can't worry about what people will or won't think." Ettie knew Nell was worried about what Abraham's brother, Simon, would think; it wasn't long enough since she'd buried Abraham. And Jennifer was likely to voice her disapproval as well.

CHAPTER 25

A FEW DAYS later Ettie made Elsa-May go with her, back to the park behind the library. A quiet picnic in the fresh air under the shade of the trees...that was what she believed they needed. Ettie spread out a cloth on the table. When she'd finished, Elsa-May picked up the picnic basket, placed it on the table, sat down and proceeded to pull out some sandwiches.

"It's a lovely day for a picnic," Ettie said as she slid onto the bench.

"It is, but I don't know how we're going to eat our way through all these sandwiches."

"Didn't I tell you?"

Elsa-May tilted her head to the side. "Didn't you tell me what?

"Jennifer is joining us." Ettie was determined to figure out if she was right about what was causing her to be so against Jedidiah.

Elsa-May's eyes bugged wide open. "I didn't know."

"There's one thing we never found out about Jedidiah."

"What's that?" Elsa-May asked.

"Who did he loan money to? I'd guess one of the people was Moses. That's why he didn't like us asking around."

"You might be right, but that's none of our business, is it? It's between Jedidiah and whomever."

Ettie cast her gaze downward. A lot of things weren't her business, but that didn't mean she didn't want to know about them. Ettie looked up to see Jennifer walking toward them. "Ah, here she is now."

Elsa-May glanced at Jennifer, and then whispered, "What are you up to, Ettie?"

"Nothing at all. I just thought Jennifer might like to have a picnic."

Jennifer greeted the ladies when she came closer and then sat down with them. "Lovely day."

"We were just talking about how nice the weather is, weren't we, Elsa-May?"

"That's right." Elsa-May offered Ettie a piercing look that Jennifer couldn't have seen as she was sitting next to Elsa-May.

Ettie placed some sandwiches on a plate and pushed them toward Jennifer. "I'm glad that dreadful business is all over for your *shweschder.*"

Jennifer took a sandwich and nodded. "Me too. I never thought things would work out between her and Jedidiah."

"You didn't care for him?" Elsa-May asked.

"*Nee,* it wasn't that, was it, Jennifer?" Ettie placed her sandwich down and looked at Jennifer.

She stared back at Ettie. "You know, don't you?"

"What would I possibly know?"

"Don't tell Nell. It'll crush her that I didn't tell her. I had to keep letting her think Jedidiah was no good for her."

Elsa-May frowned. "Why's that?"

Ettie ignored Elsa-May, and said to Jennifer, "You knew he was still alive, didn't you?"

She nodded.

Elsa-May said, "Did he contact you?"

"*Nee.*" She sighed. "I saw Titus going into the general store that day that Jedidiah disappeared, and he came out with a bundle of clothing. I had asked him to do something for me earlier that day, and he'd said he was too busy. I said he shouldn't be too busy to do something for his oldest *schweschder* and he said it was very important. Naturally, I was curious when I saw him at the general store and I followed him when he left. He headed down an alleyway and met with Jedidiah. He handed over the clothes, Jedidiah gave him money and then they shook hands. I knew he was leaving. I thought he'd just run out on her, but I could never figure out why our brother was helping him. I never knew why until the other day at your *haus.*"

"Why did you never say anything to Nell over all those years?" Ettie was pleased Jennifer had a reason to have said all those things to Nell. It wasn't that she was mean-spirited, after all.

"And what would I say? Titus was the one who knew something."

"Why didn't you ask Titus about what you saw?"

"I learned a long time ago that no good comes from prying into things."

Elsa-May then stared at Ettie and Ettie frowned at her sister.

Jennifer continued, "All I could do was be there for Nell and be her shoulder to cry on. If I could convince her that the man was never good for her and never really loved her, I hoped that would save her some pain. She was better off to think he was useless. And more so, never loved her the way he should've. I tried to get that into her brain the best I could. If I'd told her he was still alive she might never have married Abraham. She wouldn't have had her boys or her *grosskinner.*"

Elsa-May said. "You did just what any older *schweschder* might've done."

"I didn't lie. I just kept quiet. I felt awful, but once I'd made the decision to keep my lips closed, I couldn't go back on it."

"Can't be helped," Ettie said. "Now they're

going to have the happy ending they were always meant to have."

"They will," Jennifer said.

"And that's all an older *schweschder* can ask for her younger *schweschder*," Elsa-May said with a smile before she bit into her sandwich.

Ettie smiled back at Elsa-May knowing she meant well, at times. A graceful black swan gliding along the water took Ettie's attention and made her smile. As nice as the picnic was with the dappled sunlight on her skin and the gentle breeze on her face, Ettie's mind soon drifted to the Charmers. When she was sitting by the window at home, she felt better because she could keep an eye on them.

Ettie tried to push the Charmers to the back of her mind and think about Nell and Jedidiah's wedding next week. It would be a happy occasion and it was rare that two older people married.

Her mind didn't stay on the wedding for long before it drifted back to those pesky neighbors. What were they doing right now? Knocking down the fence again to blame it on Snowy, or going through their mail once more?

"Ettie!"

Ettie stared at Elsa-May. "We were talking to you and you were staring blankly at nothing."

"Oh. Was I?"

"I thought you were having a stroke." Jennifer giggled. "What were you thinking about so deeply, Ettie?"

Ettie placed her fingertip on her chin. "That a wedding is a much pleasanter event than a funeral."

Elsa-May and Jennifer looked at each other and started to giggle. Then they broke into all-out laughter. Ettie stared at them, wondering what it was they found so funny. And then she found herself laughing, too.

ETTIE SMITH AMISH MYSTERIES

ABOUT SAMANTHA PRICE

USA Today Bestselling author, Samantha Price, wrote stories from a young age, but it wasn't until later in life that she took up writing full time. Formally an artist, she exchanged her paintbrush for the computer and, many best-selling book series later, has never looked back.

Samantha is happiest on her computer lost in the world of her characters. She is best known for the Ettie Smith Amish Mysteries series and the Expectant Amish Widows series.

www.SamanthaPriceAuthor.com

Samantha loves to hear from her readers.
Connect with her at:

samantha@samanthapriceauthor.com
www.facebook.com/SamanthaPriceAuthor
Follow Samantha Price on BookBub
Twitter @ AmishRomance
Instagram - SamanthaPriceAuthor